SHORT, SHORTER AND SHORTER STORIES

Volume III

CHUCK McCANN

©2009
Nightengale Press
A Nightengale Media LLC Company

For information about Nightengale Press please
visit our website at www.nightengalepress.com.
Email: publisher@nightengalepress.com
or send a letter to:
Nightengale Press
10936 N. Port Washington Road. Suite 206
Mequon, WI 53092

Library of Congress Cataloging-in-Publication Data

McCann, Chuck

Short, Shorter and Shorter Stories, Volume III/ Chuck McCann
ISBN:1-933449-74-6
ISBN 13: 978-1933449-74-8
Short Story/Fiction
Copyright Registered: 2009
First Published by Nightengale Press in the USA

April 2009

10 9 8 7 6 5 4 3 2 1

Printed in the USA/UK

Dedication

So many stories, so many words, so much to read, so many corrections. It's a wonder my wife and daughter, Rita and Linda, say they still love me after reading them, some many times. I thank them and the casual readers of rough drafts, such as Rose and Hank and Vilma, who offer wording or clarity suggestions that I hadn't considered. I thank also teachers the world over for giving me the desire to read and the skills to collect these stories and write this book. Thank you too reader. I hope these stories, to paraphrase a certain popular movie cop, make your day.

Thank Heaven

The morning of September 3rd 1939 Rose Greene left everything she'd been promised. She sat listening as Myron Kobelman drove to the waterfront docks, while he explained as much as possible to his visiting American daughter-in-law. Upon reliable information, his business materials, supplies and bank accounts, along with many other companies' were to be seized by the government. She, an American would carry all business rights to America, hopefully keeping control should the government begin confiscation.

Aboard the small freighter, with a crew of nine men, Rose was made comfortable, albeit, hardly ever out of her cabin and unable to speak the language. It would be a nine day trip. Foul weather might add a day or two. Boredom and inactivity depressed her while the cold, damp Atlantic air had given her a violent coughing, sneezing cold and a throbbing headache. Lying in bed became too much. She also felt a bit queasy, might even have succumbed to seasickness. Dressing warmly she left her cabin and stood grimly at the ship's rail wondering if she'd die or end her suffering by throwing herself overboard.

Feeling a sneeze coming on, she frantically dug into her coat pocket. Hurrying the hankie to her face, Rose unleashed an explosive sneeze, and another and yet one more in rapid succession.

"Gesundheit," came a cheery voice from somewhere behind her.

Turning, handkerchief still pressed to her nose, Rose scanned the narrow area. In the half open doorway stood a crew member. One thought slammed into her consciousness and she spoke quickly. "Oh. Thank heaven, someone who speaks English."

The Party's Over

Looking at the head table I saw Gordon wrapping his arm around the bride and, I'm sure, whispering into her ear. She gave him a slight shove, sending him away from her and onto the dance floor. Weaving in and out he traversed from the front of the room to the open bar off in the back corner. Having watched his progress and anticipating his destination, we arrived at the bar together.

"Gordon you're drunk."

"I am? I am." He put his arm around my waist and lifted me up onto the bar. Waving his hand in the direction of the head table and the bride he said, in a sodden slur, "Ain't she pretty? Huh? Ain't she?"

"She is pretty Gordon. And you are drunk."

"Our sister, the pretty bride."

"Gordon, they're leaving in a minute or two. The party is over." I shifted my weight and lowered myself from my perch. "It's time for everyone to go home. You too."

"Time to go home?"

The bartender was directly behind us waiting, I would guess, to see how I was going to handle Gordon. I do believe he would have helped me if I had asked for help.

At five foot two and 98 pounds, I thought I could handle my 6 foot 200 pound brother. "Gordon you're drunk. Give me your car keys." My empty hand, palm up, waited at his chest level and the keys fell into it. "Thank you."

"Welcome."

"Let's go," I said tugging at his elbow and heading for the exit.

"Night," the bartender called from behind me. "Drive careful."

"Will do. Night."

I poked at Gordon until he was in the car, albeit, slouched in the seat like a package of cleaning. I got in, started the engine and ground the gears as I shifted and pulled out onto a nearly empty street. The car was adjusted for brother Gordon which made my driving a little difficult. First I was a little too far to the left, then to the right, and back left again. Stopping at the stoplight, I killed the engine. When I started out with the green light, I ground the gears and killed the engine. Gordon was sawing lumber unaware of my predicament.

Soon enough things came together and I proceeded down our street. The siren behind me as I stopped in front of the house paralyzed my senses. Why did the police pull up behind me? I started to move but the engine died. The police officer turned off the siren and was out of his car walking toward me.

"Oh," he said.

"Oh," I said.

"How are you Doris?" asked Officer Ron Hunt, Gordon's closest friend and my present pursuer.

"Fine Ron. Just fine," I mumbled. "You after me or did you recognize Gordon's car?"

Leaning down he looked over to the bulk occupying the front seat. "Gordon?"

"Gordon, drunk and out of it."

"Hey. You're all dressed up and Gordon's smashed. Sister's wedding, huh?"

"Uh huh. They're off on their honeymoon and the three of us are here."

Putting his finger into the collar of his shirt, Ron tugged, loosening the fabric around his Adam's apple. "Well I didn't recognize the car when I stopped you. Thought I had a drunk driver not a drunk passenger. You were weaving all over the street."

"I was, wasn't I?"

"Yeah. You know if someone else had stopped you they'd have given you a ticket and may even have taken your driver's license away."

"No they wouldn't."

Ron tugged at his collar again, "Believe me, another guy would do just that."

"Can't."

"Come on. Why not?"

"I don't have a driver's license."

An astonished look crept across Ron's face. "You can't drive without a license." I thought he'd fall down as he started laughing at my answer.

"I can't drive. I don't know how."

A Pair of New Glasses

Armour stood staring into the box while exploring the contents with his fingers wondering if there was a pair of eyeglasses in there for him. He'd been told that some kids already were given glasses and they could see things much better since they put them on. He couldn't resist the temptation. Even though he'd been told not to touch he reached in and carefully took out a large pair. He didn't care about the frame color or shape in his selection, for him that wasn't important. Adjusting them on the bridge of his nose and over his ears, he moved his head about, noticing no significant change in what he usually saw.

"Armour, I told you not to touch any of the eyeglasses in that box," came the terse order of the man entering the room.

"I know, Dr. Paul. I just wanted to see if they work," Armour said, replacing the glasses into the box.

"They work fine, but not for blind people like you."

The Monkey Paw Trap

Chattering in fright and jumping about to avoid capture, the little monkey remained trapped by the jar tied to a stake. He provided the hunter with his next meal. Did the monkey give its life for greed or ignorance? You decide.

The native hunter tied a narrow necked pot to a cord fastened to a stake. He then shoved a piece of root just a bit smaller than the neck into the pot. He made sure the monkeys in the surrounding trees saw the root go into the pot.

The hunter then hid nearby and watched the trap. He didn't wait long. The monkey's arm probed the inside of the pot, found the root and clutching it, found its arm was locked in the trap. A predicament. It saw the hunter advancing and began the struggle for freedom. We know the ending here.

Bruno Vincent, a.k.a. "Viney" Vincent, stood before the warden at the prison gate. The small man, often mistaken for a jockey, wouldn't look up into the warden's eyes. He held his clasped hands in front of him, his eyes studying the shiny twinkles of broken glass caught in a crack of the pavement. It was late Monday morning.

"You're out Bruno, see if you can stay out. Another trip here could last a long time."

"OK, Warden. I'll try not to get caught. Ah, er, to come back," said Bruno.

"Don't come back, Bruno. I mean it," said the warden. "Open up Roy. He's outta here."

"Yes, sir." The button was pushed, the motor overhead whirred and the gate slid along its track. Bruno stepped into a free world. Three "Byes" bounced out of a nearby doorway. Bruno didn't look back.

Bruno had a side interest, birding. He was too lazy to run to a park or beach looking for birds with his binoculars because someone might accuse him of being a Peeping Tom. Bruno sat in his room and focused on roof tops, telephone poles and wires. He could safely and lazily watch the birds. Oh, he occasionally looked through a few windows too.

Bruno's eyes grew wide when he happened to focus on the third floor window at the end of an alley just two blocks over. Through the window, in plain view, there was a jewelry repair shop. He spent more time looking through that window than at the mating dance of a proud pigeon on the flat roof next door. He made some mental notes about the outside of the building and the fact that the window had bars. He also carefully studied the habits of the man sitting directly in front of the barred window and how close he worked to the window. While Bruno couldn't squeeze through the bars on the window his arm could.

This man was careless, sloppy and his workbench cluttered. Loose gold and silver wire just placed on shelves, gem stones likewise near a little *open* lockbox. This observation nearly caused Bruno to wet his pants, it wasn't fastened down. The man actually pushed it around the workbench when he wanted more working space. Bruno let out a long soft whistle when he saw this. If his eyes didn't glow then they glowed later.

Later was closing time. This idiot left everything on his workbench when he went home after work. Everything? Well, he did put a nice stone in the box one night. Bruno wasn't positive he locked the box, or if it locked at all. He began dreaming, night and day, of getting some jewelry. Carefully he checked the outside of the building, the window and the edge of the roof, he couldn't see more than that.

All day Thursday, Bruno kept his glasses on the little repair shop. Yesterday he had walked down the alley. Under the window of the repair shop he stopped. For many minutes he looked up, his eyes combing the wall, searching for any weakness. He found one, a big one. About every eighteen inches the builder had indented a row of bricks. The pattern added dimension to the drabness of a red brick wall.

Bruno glanced around and saw no one. He placed his fingers in the created groove. He placed his shoe in another groove. He pulled himself up. He quickly stepped down, patted the wall, and, while walking quickly away, kissed his hand. A Human Fly could climb that wall, he was sure of that. Well so could he.

The moon was blocked behind a cloudy sky. Streetlights cast vague shadows close to the alley entrance. Bruno stopped at the entrance. With furtive glances this way and that, he darted into the shadows. Moments later he was scaling the wall. In minutes he braced his body against the wall, holding tightly to the bars on the window. He slipped his arm between the bars and felt his heartbeat go into double time, no, triple time as his fingers touched the clutter on the workbench.

"BINGO!" He almost hollered it. Almost. His hand encircled the small lockbox. "DAMN!" He almost hollered. Almost. His foot slipped out of the groove. His body fell as the other hand jerked away from the window bar. The hand around the little box remained shut, smashed against the window bars. His body torqued about putting his back to the wall. He could feel deep pain in the shoulder of the arm caught in between the bars. He may have broken something in the arm.

Now three floors up, dangling in space with a possible broken something, Bruno had some decisions to make. With really no time to dwell on any decision for a long time, he began thinking. First, the hand holding the box was holding him snugly, if he opens his hand he loses the lock box, which he wants. Two, if he opens his hand he will fall and perhaps severely injure himself. Three, he could holler for help and lose everything, because the newspeople would show up with their TV cameras. Caught between the devil and a hard spot, he made his choice.

Watching the news, the crowd in the hospital corridor laughed loudly and the squad room crowd at the police station did too, as they watched the firemen clambering up the ladder to Bruno. The flood light beams knitted the scene together for all to see. Bruno hanging by one arm was shivering but very still. He was screaming curses at the slowness of the rescue team. But he didn't twitch a muscle. His held tight to the little box until the fireman pried the hand open.

Someone in the crowd of gawkers said, "Poor little monkey."

What Did You Say Your Name Was?

I know you. We were introduced at ah... At ahh... Oh, you know. What's 'er name. The gal with the twins. Or does she have three boys? But, you know who I mean. Don't you? Anyway, we met there. It was just a week or so ago. But I've forgotten. What did you say your name was?

You look familiar. I saw you across the room and right away I knew I knew you.

But where or how? I pointed you out to my spouse. 'Sorry, don't know.' Big help!

But I do know you. I just have to remember from where. You look like a relative of mine. You're not? Are you? You also look like that actor. What's the name? Oh, hell! What did you say your name was?

Sorry, but I wasn't paying attention when you were introduced. I enjoyed your presentation. 'Lots of interesting points.' I liked your comparison of ancient lifestyles to modern couples. Do you feel people really enjoy stuff prepared that way? What? You didn't mean it that way? Oh! You weren't the speaker on that subject? 'Sorry!' It was a good topic. What did you say your name was?

So, do you remember? We met last night, at the church social. You came with someone from out of town. We sat at the corner table. You said you weren't feeling so hot and your date wasn't around. "Could I drive you home?" you asked. When we got there, I stayed to see if you were going to be OK. I guess I fell asleep afterwards. After?

Yeah, after! Sure we did. Do I respect you? Sure. I'm leaving now. Call you? Yeah.

Sure. What did you say you name was?

Who are you? Why are you dressing me? And, who are the people you're talking about? I don't know an Aimee. I had a doll years ago I called Aimee. But she's lost I guess. Did I have breakfast yet? I know put my arm in. OK, it's in! Why are you taking my shoes away and whose slippers are those? They feel comfortable. Can you tell me about the people in the picture on the dresser? I don't know who you mean. The little one is your daughter. My grand daughter? Mary Anne! I think my mother's name was Mary Anne. I wonder where she is? Thank you! I appreciate your help. Bye! What did you say your name was?

A Different Point of View

"Don't park where a security camera might see us."

"OK, Mike. I'll be careful. I'll look for the camera and park away from it."

After the robbery Donald and Mike drove to their apartment and threw their loot on the table. Grabbing a cold beer for each of them, Donald sat down as Mike started counting out their share. Neither moved as the shattering door parts showered around them and armed policemen stormed into the room.

Shocked, bewildered and handcuffed, Mike sat in the back of the squad car, begging for an explanation. "How'dya know so quick? Huh? How? Come on tell me. Please."

"OK, stupid, I'll tell you. But understand you're both real asses. The security camera caught you running to your car," the officer sitting in the front seat of the squad car said.

"Bullshit. You're lying. We parked where the security cameras aren't posted."

"Not from the security camera across the street."

Benjamin's Check

"Where you off to?" Tiny asked Benjamin as he walked through the pool hall toward the street.

"Well I haven't anything special in mind. Thought I might catch a streetcar and go down to the Loop, see what's happening, wander around. It's free day at the Art Institute, I could go there."

"You were at the museum a week or two ago, wasn't you?"

"Yeah," Benjamin agreed, "But I like the place and the pictures. Who can tell, maybe some day I might own one of them and donate it to the Institute. Then every day would be a free day for me."

"Dreamer. I got some work for you tonight, think you can be here by seven?"

"OK."

Benjamin moved in behind the Cottage Grove streetcar and grabbed the holder for the rope that controlled the trolley rod with the electrical wires overhead. His free ride ended at 71st Street when the conductor shagged him off with a holler. So Benjamin continued his walk along the street. As he passed the cemetery fortune smiled upon him. Lying in the street was a small leather folder, not old and not new, but worn with use.

Scooping it up, Benjamin found it to be an old checkbook, empty of checks, with a few old deposit slips and two old receipts. It was a thin line of pale green between the receipts that caught his eye. Wonder of wonders Benjamin mused at his sudden turn of good luck. A check. A blank check snuggled between the two scraps of paper. Oh, this set his mind whirling with ideas, each idea making him richer and richer. He kissed the check before slipping it into his shirt pocket and flipped the now empty folder over the cemetery fence.

Benjamin headed for Sears on 79th Street. His mind had devised a scheme that would get him a few bucks courtesy of, he plucked the check from his pocket and read the name on the check aloud, "Courtesy of Mr. Albert K. Chambers." Carefully he returned the check to the pocket, and then went over his plan. He went over it several times before he walked into the store.

In the store Benjamin quite casually moved to the section containing office supplies. His interest was the Remington typewriters on display. They were out, usually with some paper, for customers to test their ease and quality and possibly purchase. He had a different use in mind. Looking around, the single sales clerk was on the other side of the aisle from the typewriters busy with a customer. Benjamin stepped up to the typewriter, saying to himself,

"Slip the check in and line it up. Good, good. The date, April first, nineteen forty-seven." Looking around, he continued talking, *"Type in your name and the amount. Remember don't get greedy. Make it for, for one hundred and twenty dollars."*

Taking a quick look he extracted the check from behind the roller and placed it back in his pocket. Next stop the currency exchange back on the Grove. He felt rather smug strolling instead of walking west along 79th Street. Several times he peeked into his pocket reassuring himself that the check was still there.

In the currency exchange he stepped up to the counter as the only other patron stepped away. He endorsed the back of the check and went straight to the cashier's window. Sliding the check through the tray under the thick glass he waited for the man to count out his money.

"How you doing?" he inquired of the man, now giving Benjamin a look.

"Fine." With a crooked half-assed grin he asked, "Want anything else?"

"No. Just my money. Thanks."

The coins slid with a clink into the metal tray.

Bewildered by the sound Benjamin waited for the paper bills to follow.

"Something else?" the cashier asked Benjamin, still standing at the window.

"Well, sure. The rest of my money."

"That's all you get. We charge two-bits, twenty-five cents for cashing a check. You get ninety-five cents, three quarters, two dimes."

"But, but. I just gave you a check from my uncle, Mr. Albert K. Chambers, for one hundred twenty dollars. He just paid me for the work I been doing at his house."

The man picked up the check that Benjamin had passed to him. Shaking his head he said, "Go back to your uncle and have him write you a new check." He retrieved the coins from the slot and slid Benjamin's check back to him. "Look at the amount kid. It says, one dollar twenty cents."

Benjamin's eyes focused on the amount he had so carefully typed. He saw instead not the $120. he wanted to type, but $1.20. He misplaced the decimal point and the money he wanted.

Oh Deer Me

Grace's face became ashen and her eyes fluttered before she collapsed onto the floor. Slim expected this to happen but his reflexes were not quick enough. The solid thud he heard made him wince as her head hit the floor.

"Grady, you home? I need some help," Slim hollered toward the rooms in the back of the house. He'd often been in the house as a friend and co-worker of Grace's husband Dave Flood, game warden. He heard the back bedroom door open and shouted, "Stop in the john and bring a wet towel."

"OK. OK. What's happening Slim? Where's mom?"

"Right here. Bring that wet towel."

Grady came into the room faster than a runaway express train, falling down next to his mom as he endeavored to stop. "Oh, God." He gulped and repeated, "Oh God. God."

"She fainted, that's all boy." Placing the wet towel on her forehead Slim directed, "Hold this here." He got up and went to the cabinet next to the TV and removed a bottle of whiskey. "We'll both need this."

Grace moaned and stirred then opened her gray eyes to see Grady' face looking into hers. The clink of the bottle hitting the glass turned her head toward Slim. Her confused look changed into fear as Slim stepped into her field of vision. She remembered.

"Take this Grace," handing her the glass he'd just poured. He drank from the bottle.

The whiskey burning its way down her throat created the contorted wrinkles in her face. Grace, with Grady assisting, sat up but remained on the floor. She clutched him close and sobbed.

Bewildered, Grady's facial expression begged for information, "What....What happened?"

Slim began speaking, but Grace cut him off. "Gimme a minute."

"Sure."

"Slim, you sure? Positive?"

"Yes Grace. Positive. I was right there in the... in the..."

"Grady your Dad's in the hospital, hurt. You can come with us to the hospital or go over to Ben's and I'll call you to tell you what's what later."

"I'll go with you," the fourteen year old said.

Slim opened the hospital emergency room door before the whining of the siren died completely. His uniform prioritized his position at the registration desk getting immediate attention.

"If you're with the officer they brought in," she said, "Emergency bay C," pointing through the panel doors to her right. "C."

"Thanks," Grace muttered aloud chasing after Slim and trailed by Grady.

A disembodied head opened the door of the small waiting room, "Mrs. Flood?"

"Yes."

"I'm Dr. Levee. I just attended your husband."

Anxious beyond her capacity to control herself, Grace broke in, "Is he OK?"

Stopped by her question, he pursed his lips before shaking his head in the negative. "He lost so much blood before he got here..."

Grady, assuming he could ask, after all they were talking about his father, said, "Is my father dead?"

A positive nod, a quiet yes and a heart wrenching wail echoed beyond the walls of the waiting room. A friend, a husband, a father and a patient had just died.

Three weeks later the coroner's report was read by the Court Clerk for the record. As she finished reading and sat down, those attending the hearing realized that Game Warden David Flood had died as a result of being stabbed several times by the antlers of a deer. It became apparent when testimony and photographs were submitted after the autopsy, that David thought he was checking the carcass of a dead deer. Upon grabbing the antlers, probably to turn the animal, the animal revived and attacked David, killing him. Verdict, accidental death.

Eventually Slim was informed that the frozen carcass of the deer, no longer to be kept as evidence in David's death, was to be burned in the incinerator next morning. He was requested to assist with the job because one man could not handle every detail by himself.

Since David's death Slim frequently stopped at the Flood house. Grace was quite grateful to see him, often asking that he stay for dinner, and just as often he was leaving the house in the late hours. At first Grady enjoyed the visits, but mentioned to his mother that people might talk about their guest.

"They're burning that damn deer carcass tomorrow. Gotta help."

"I didn't know they kept those things," said Grace, placing the roast on the table.

"Do and don't. Sometimes it's a year or two, even longer. Other times, gone the next day." Slim cut into the deer roast, part of an animal confiscated from a poacher. "How big a slice you want Grady?" he asked. "Evidence they no longer need usually gets torched."

"Slim, do they burn it all."

"All."

"If you ask them, would they maybe not burn the antlers so I could have them?"

"Grady," Grace interjected. "Why do you want the antlers? Those things killed your father. I won't have them in the house. Besides you have the set your father gave you hanging in your room."

"I don't want to keep them in the house. I want to chop them up."

"Grady," Slim put his hand on the boy's shoulder, "bad idea. Listen to mom."

"And I don't want any arguing about it," Grace added. "None."

The following evening Slim called Grady over as he exited his car at the Flood house. "Got a little something for you. Never tell your mom what it is or where you got it. And get rid of it somewhere away from the house as quick as possible." He handed the boy a tissue wrapped object no bigger than a peach pit. "It's the piece of antler they removed from your father during the autopsy."

"How did you get it?"

"No questions. Put it somewhere then get rid of it. OK?"

"Mom, after supper can I go to the quarry with Freddy?"

"It's not a safe place to be in the evening."

"I just wanna see if we can...can set up some rocks for sitting tomorrow. Remember the fishing tournament starts tomorrow. You said I could be in it."

"Do you have to do it tonight?"

"We can fish longer if we do it tonight. Right Slim?" Grady patted his pocket, a signal to Slim that the object was there.

"Let him go Grace, I'm sure they won't be gone long."

Freddy's father looked up from his tackle box as the two boys walked passed the open door. "Where you two going?"

"The quarry. We're going to get ready for the fishing tournament tomorrow."

"Well that's nice. I was just putting these mini-lures in my tackle box. Now I'm thinking I'll go with you and try these new mini-lures tonight. Mind? I'll stay away from your spot."

"OK, Dad. It's OK, ain't it Grady?"

"You already said it was."

At the quarry Grady pulled the wad of tissue from his pocket. "I wanna smash this thing first."

"Smash what? What thing?" asked Freddy.

"Slim told me it's part of the antler from the deer that killed my Dad. I'm gonna smash it to pieces with a rock and throw it in the quarry."

As he unwrapped the tissue Freddy's father reappeared. "I just broke my rod tip."

Surprised, Grady dropped the partially unwrapped tissue from his hand. Picking it up Freddy's father twisted it between finger and thumb. "Piece of muley antler. I haven't seen mule deer antlers since leaving my ranger job in California. You didn't just find it here, did you boys?"

"No Dad," Freddy said, "it's a piece from the deer that..." He stopped talking, realizing that he was saying something he shouldn't. He was right, Grady was furious.

"I'd like it back, please," the boy said coldly. He extended his hand.

"Grady," The man could see the anger and determination in the boy's eyes. "Grady, what are you going to do with this?"

"Smash it."

"Oh, it's not a souvenir?"

"No. That deer killed my father. I want to smash it like it smashed my father."

"I see. You know this type of antler isn't found around here."

"Sure it is. Slim said it came from the deer that killed my Dad. He kept it from being burned today when they burned the old evidence."

"Grady, I think we have a mystery here. A very big mystery. Let's solve it before you smash this piece of bone. Please."

Grady ran through the house prompting his mother to holler, "Grady, stop running in the house."

"I gotta get something for Officer Bail. He's coming from his car now." Back he came, running and carrying the set of antlers from his room. Officer Bail had just stepped onto the front porch when Grady handed him the set of antlers. Grace and Slim stepped out to meet him.

"Hi Paul, what's the commotion?" Slim asked.

"I really don't know." The officer turned to Freddy and his father now walking up the walk toward the house. "It seems these antlers might..."

Grace reached out to retrieve the antlers, "I'll take those."

"No ma'am, you will not," the officer replied.

"Problem?" inquired Slim, his arm wrapped around Grace's waist.

"Problem. Grady, you say these were a gift to you from your father?"

"He gave them to me a couple of years ago. They're mine."

"Will you give them to me now?"

"Not for keeps."

"No not for keeps. You'll get them back."

With all the evidence burned, except for a piece of antler, blood on a set of antlers and some photographs from old editions of the local paper showing the white-tailed deer that killed David

Flood, a case was built for a trial of Grace Flood and Slim Tuttle. The two had rendezvoused behind David's back and finally had decided to kill him. Slim hit him with a tree branch then stabbed him with the souvenir antlers of Grady's. After the killing the antlers were wiped off and hung back in the boy's room, no one the wiser. Slim's little gesture to win over the boy proved to be pointless.

The God's Gifts

Long ago, before time began, the gods of man discussed the idea that man should have to live in harmony with the creatures the gods had put on Earth for his happiness.

The gods wished to nurture man and gave him a share of their feelings; pride, happiness, strength, conceit, faith and self-importance. However with just these feelings man would be a god and this could not be.

They met and bickered until all agreed. Man would have the opposite feeling of each feeling he now knew. They almost overdid their gift, for often man wished he never had these opposites. When man complained, the gods were furious and talk soon filled the heavens to destroy this undeserving and insignificant mortal, this toy.

Fortunately for us, they didn't.

When the gods gave man a mate called woman, for she was drawn from the belly of man, they also gave her feelings. It was agreed by the gods that woman's feelings, while the same as man's, would often be more profound, sillier, less important or in some way different than man's. Poor man. Poor woman. What they often felt they could not share, what they both felt was often shared and neither understood how this could be.

This gift the gods called The Battle of the Sexes. The battle is not resolved yet, to the merriment of the gods.

Man's feelings run deep and somber, flamelessly burning his soul. He feels his strength, built on years of practice and natural abilities, can provide everything he and woman need to survive. He forgets his unquestioned gifts. Woman meanwhile believes in his abilities. She does not question him aloud, but prays he understands that she is there and will share and help when he beckons. Together they can achieve their goals.

However they are not alone. For wisdom, a godly attribute often unknown to man or woman, gave other men and women the desire to help. It is this feeling, between choice and faith, that allows hope to grow when shared.

The gods decreed long before the bones of time became dust, that each species give to the next a token of themselves. This would be an everlasting memory. Millennia have passed and man continues giving the token. We take pride in giving and seeing the gift accepted. The ability to accept warms all in the circle of family or friends.

Unfathomed is the wisdom of the gods and we are wise not to question it.

That's Life

"Chip, you're a good man. A God fearing man and a brave man." The heavyset man sat comfortably in the verandah chair looking down on the slightly built black man standing in the dirt at the bottom of the steps. "I know you are the best harness maker in the area and I truly need your services. However, I think you would work for me if I asked you."

The black man nodded in affirmation.

"Knew you would. I can never thank you enough for carrying my grandson out of the house last night. The way the flames swept through the place didn't offer much hope of the boy surviving. By the way, are your burns paining you?"

"Some Sir. The kitchen woman greased them good and tied some clean cloth on them."

"Good. Good." For a moment the man said nothing, peering into the distance then drawing a deep breath continued speaking.

"You will have your freedom by late this afternoon. I have the parson writing papers for you."

The negro started raising his hand as if dismissing the words he had just heard, though the action was unneeded, and instead nodded his head. For twenty seven years he spoke only when asked to speak or confirm what was said. This was 1850 America, Bayonne, Carolina and he was a slave. He knew his place.

"This is little I dare say but I consider you a free man now. Papers will allow you to travel and work as you please." The rocking chair squeaked as the man rode with his thoughts beyond the verandah. Silence from him and the standing man, the humming from the bees while they worked the morning glories climbing the surrounding banisters was the only sound. When his thoughts returned Ben Shell began speaking again, "You may stay on here as long as you need a place. Even eat with the other workers if it pleases you."

Chip knew he was being asked to reply. "For today Sir. I'll stay for the day and clean up the harness shop for your new man. Do you want Matthew to take over in there? He works well, I know he does."

"Yes. Since you're staying a bit, bring him up here to the house after the dinner's been served."

"That I will do Sir."

"You go along now Chip. Do what e're you please, you're a free man now."

That night Chip had taken Matthew to the house and it was confirmed that he would take Chip's place as the harness maker. Chip was also given his paper declaring him a free man. Now the two men sat at the work bench discussing Chip's options for the future. As they talked Chip frequently rubbed his belt containing his paper. Many years ago he made the belt cleverly crafting a pouch into it to hold his treasures. It held his greatest treasure now, a piece of folded paper that told everyone he was a free man.

"Matthew, you know I have a full Christian name now."

"That being what Chip?"

"Why man, you can figure that out." He rubbed his hand over the pouch in the belt. "I am a free man, a free man. My name is Chip Freeman. Sounds so good, I'll keep saying it in my sleep tonight. Chip Freeman."

"Don't that be something. Chip Freeman. I like your new name." Matthew tightened a piece of tanned cow hide in the clamp, "Thought I'd take this scrap and make me a belt like yours. Whatta you think of that?"

"I think you should buy the leather before using it. Don't make troub..."

A small boy ran up, "Mr. Chip, I'm to ask you to come up to the house soon as poss...poss..." A gasp stopped his message. "Can you come now?"

"Young one, you shouldn't interrupt when men are talking."

"Sorry."

"Master Shell asking for me?"

"Been someone or another at the house all day." Sucking in another gulp of air, "Might be someone knowing you are a free man has work for you."

"Well I'll walk back with you. And Matthew, save yourself trouble." Taking the boy's shoulder he turned him around and gently propelled him through the door. "Let us go up to the house."

Approaching the house, the youngster bolted forward hollering, "He's here!"

The man sitting in the shade of the verandah rocking gently waved and called to the boy, "Thank you, Albert. Now you get back an' help your momma in the kitchen." Chip stopped at the steps and waited, hat in hand behind his back. "Chip," said the man quietly rivaling the chorus frogs of a nearby pond as he returned to rocking. "I have been told there is a load o' hides down on the dock waiting to be shipped to France. They wait to be loaded because the tax hasn't been paid. Would you go and look at these hides? Take this letter of purchase with you and if they're good and the tax hasn't been paid see the Harbor Master to buy them, but at a reasonable price, and bring them here."

"You wish me to buy them at the price I think or the tax price?"

"You fox. Get them at the best price." He leaned back into the rocker laughing loudly, wiping the heel of his hand into the flow of tears the laughter produced. "The best price. And I'm sure I'll get the better bargain from you."

"I will do my best."

"I know." The once sparkling eyes, dimmed by time, looked at the paper in his hand, "This is the letter of purchase. It is good as gold. I needn't tell you to keep it safe."

"I'll put in a safe place," and a twinkle came into his eye. "You remember which is my safe place?"

A gnarled finger pointed to Chip's left shoe. "I remember how good you work."

And Chip remembered the old man knew of one safe place, his shoe, not his belt. Taking the paper and folding it, he leaned down and slipped it between a fold of leather. "I'll take the wagon and go at once. Should I take someone with me?"

"No need, there are men on the dock that'll help you. Take care now."

The creaking of the wagon and the dull thud of the horse's hooves alerted the figure walking in the middle of the road. The early morning dew had already lifted and dust began to rise from the road. Chip didn't recognize the man peering up at him as he drove by. While it was customary to offer a ride Chip thought twice about it and continued driving toward town. He felt the pull of the wagon gate as the man thrust his body into the wagon bed. Turning to face the intruder he was struck by a powerful fist that closed out the light of the morning.

The stranger sat on the wagon seat popping the reins on the horse's back to keep him moving. The animal was unfamiliar with the stranger's touch and the road he had turned onto. The driver, in a bit of a hurry to move away from town, kept the horse moving but thought about the changes he was experiencing since he woke that morning.

Elyria Oat's hand scooped water from the horse trough onto his face. He squinted his eyes to close out the early morning sunlight and wished for a drink. Of course the brew he swilled into the late hours of yesterday was the reason he felt miserable at the moment. He knew no one in town, had not a cent and looked and smelled like flotsam beached in a storm. For now, Oats avoided walking near people, or rather they avoided Oats by stepping quickly aside as he moved passed them. He soon reached the wharf and settled on a protruding piling and began thinking of a means to come by some money or a method of obtaining food.

Fortune tipped her hand in his favor as two men carrying fish they were unloading from a small boat, dropped one at his feet as they jogged along the planks. Oats was quick to recover the shiny glazed-eyed creature. Tucking it beneath his coat he headed up the broad sands of the beach. Driftwood provided the fuel for his fire and he soon picked at the charred flesh, more burnt than cooked, from the wooden spit he'd pierced through the fish.

Belching his pleasure, he headed toward the wooded area to finish his toilet then proceeded back into town. Heading toward the stables he considered, as he had in the past, requesting some work cleaning the stalls and removing the manure to the ever present pile located behind the building. He was soon sweating at honest labor and keeping his eyes open for an opportunity to grab something to steal and hide under the pile to recover after nightfall.

A bridle hanging just beside the door of the tack room caught his eye and, as beautiful as it was, it disappeared under the fresh pile of manure for later.

Three other items joined it before the day was finished. Elyria informed the stable owner he wouldn't be back tomorrow. He took his coins and went to seek comfort with a wretched bottle of brew purchased on the wharf.

A dog barked and a man swore as Elyria, with no recourse, dug with his bare hands under the edge of the manure pile to claim his stolen goods. The remainder of the night he spent on the beach waiting for morning to clean his goods and examine them more closely. After washing them he set out at once along the road for the next town. It was possible that someone might recognize the things he had and make trouble for him here.

He found a buyer, but the buyer recognized the bridle and threatened to call the authorities. Sans the loot, Elyria ran down the road then slipped into the woods to avoid any pursuers and to catch his breath.

As the sky darkened and the pale stars brightened overhead the bumping jolting ride stopped. Elyria Oats swung around on the seat, as he had done frequently for hours, to ascertain the condition of the man he had attacked. Looking down into the open but bewildered eyes, he winked. "Looks like I trussed up a runaway darkie." Another wink, "You got a name darkie?"

Chip had been awake since the bumps, jolts and pain had revived his aching head. Attempted movement to ease his discomfort was useless. His legs and arms were bound tight. When he awoke the clouds were tinged with a light blush of pink, indicating he was moving westward away from the sea, from home. Trying to yell he found his jaw stiff and painful, unable to open even a bit. In this condition he considered it best to await the driver's decision about his future. He prayed to the Almighty God that this would not be his last day on earth. Now this man wanted his name and he couldn't give it, but he nodded yes, he had a name.

"You dumb or my punch bust your mouth?" The smile breaking the man's face was a sneer, one that actually frightened Chip. A rough hand seized his jaw, twisting it up toward the sneer.

"AAAAAAgghhhhhhhh!" broke from Chip's mouth.

"Guess I broke it, huh?" Another twist, another scream. "Yep. Busted it."

Tears overflowing from Chip's eyes ran down into his ears. Fearing the worst he forced his mind to pray, *"Forgive me God, but I wish You to damn this man, this beast to hell."*

Shifting his weight Elyria positioned himself to step down from the wagon. Pausing he said, "Stay right there, I'll be back for you," patting the tear stained cheek.

Chip lay still. His hands and feet once numb from the tight ropes now hurt and his jaw throbbed. He could go nowhere. The reddening glow of a fire gleamed from the nail heads in the bottom of the wagon seat and the twinkling stars shone more brightly. The sound of walking on gravel and twigs, the clink of metal against metal kept Chip aware of the man's presence. Worry and prayer filled his time. Hunger gave his stomach a voice.

The soft thud, thud, thud of horse hooves woke Chip. They seemed to be approaching, he wasn't sure. The glow on the nail head was gone and the stars had shifted position. *"Please Lord let it be someone coming to help me. Please."* He sensed someone moving passed the wagon and waited.

"You, get up." The order was loud and direct. "Hold your hands out where I can see them."

Elyria sleepily peered up at a rifle barrel resting on his forehead held by a giant from his position on the ground. Very slowly he placed his hands out from his fetal position, palms open. Still unclear of everything happening, the alcohol consumed before falling asleep made thinking slow, he sat up. A man on horseback came close to the confused man.

"Who are you and why are you here?"

Looking up, and coming awake now, the sitting man replied in a husky whiskey voice, "Elyria Oats. I'm waiting till morning to keep going. I ain't bothering no one Sir."

"We'll see. Just you stay sitting." Turning in his saddle he gave a low whistle, a signal to unseen companions. "Calvin, see what he has there," pointing to a small bundle the sleeper used as a pillow.

The bundle received a slight kick and disgorged a nearly empty bottle. Calvin didn't even pick it up, "Just a bit of whiskey in a bottle."

"Look in the wagon too."

He stepped up on the wheel hub and fell back awkwardly to the ground. "My God there's a man in there. Looks all tied up."

Drawing his weapon the horseman hollered, "You in the wagon, stand up with your hands up."

Chip heard the order, but could not comply.

Calvin, now back on his feet said, "I think he's tied."

"You're not sure? Stand up fellow."

"That's a runaway slave I got tied up in there," Elyria said. "Don't go shooting him and costing me my reward."

The horseman moved his mount close to the wagon, peering in he asked, "You a runaway?" The man was looking at him, without a gag, yet didn't answer. "Are you?"

"I busted his jaw when I wrestled him down to capture him. Can't talk now."

The signaled riders came to the site. There were five men now. A bit puzzled by what they saw, they waited for orders.

The apparent leader did just that, "Two of you men get in there and take that fellow out. See what else is in there too." They lifted Chip handing him to Calvin who leaned him against the wagon. He promptly fell to the ground his numb legs too weak to support him. Calvin assisted him to his feet. The two men were face to face as Calvin held him, each knowing somehow they knew each other, but, unsure, they said nothing.

"Anyone recognize this," coughing interrupted him, "reputed runaway?" All five men looked, shook their heads and stepped back from the wagon.

At this point Oats screwed up his courage saying, "Sir, I think you should be telling me why you're busying with me and my property."

"Mind yourself my fellow." Sliding from his saddle he walked to the glowing embers and hunkering down extended his hands over the warmth. He raised one hand as if expecting Elyria Oats to speak again. Oats maintained his position and silence. The squatting man, pushing his hands against his legs, rose and faced Oats. "We are the Guardians. We roam the roads some nights patrolling for thieves of horses, cattle and slaves. Now tell me about yourself and how you come," he flicked the quirt he had drawn from a pocket of his jacket, "by his man."

Chip issued an audible sigh and licking his lips pulled his hands into a position indicating he wanted a drink. Calvin, looking about, saw none. "You," speaking to Elyria, "Have you water?"

"Nope. Whiskey, in the bottle there."

Looking back to Chip, he got a nod of refusal.

"OK Mr. Oats, tell us your story. One of you men set some wood to burning."

Burning embers and smoke twisted upward as he started speaking. "Like I told you my name is Elyria Oats. I arrived, let me think, three days back, by ship. I used my savings to buy this wagon hoping to hire out but ain't found a load yet. You can see it's empty. So I started out of town thinking I could get something to cart in. You know, garden goods maybe."

"Well and good. And your prisoner? How did you come by him?"

"I bought some whiskey and read the notices on the wall. I saw this here darkie lurking in the woods and remembered reading one notice which fitted him. I hollered for him to come out and he ran. So I ran after him and jumped him. He fought me and then I hit him hard and down he went. Busted his jaw then."

"Guess you did. So why have you stopped here?"

"It was getting late and after I tied his hands I hustled him into the wagon and tied his feet. It made me tired so I camped for the night. I'll have him back in town for the reward in the morning."

Turning, the man walked over to Chip and Calvin. "Can you hold yourself up now? I wish to talk, private with Calvin." Placing his arm over Calvin's shoulder they moved off before Chip could even answer. He grabbed the wheel for support and stood trembling, watching them walk away.

"Calvin, we can't stay here all night, other roads need checking. I'm not sure of this man so I want you to stay here 'til morning. First light you take them and the wagon in to the army officer..."

"Lt. Trump?"

"Yes, Trump. Tell him what we found and let him handle it." They had returned to the wagon, "Mount up, we've things to do," he said, mounting his own horse. "See you later Cal." With a wave of his arm the riders rode off into the darkness.

Calvin dropped some bits of wood on the fire. Looking at both men he said, "Oats, you help that man over here to the fire. Then we're all going to wait for sunrise."

"I don't," he stopped as Calvin waved his hand indicating he wasn't going to listen. Trying to avoid touching Chip and hold him so he could walk, Elyria stumbled back toward the burning fire. Once more Chip gazed into the face of his rescuer as they passed. At that moment Calvin knew who he was. Without a word he delivered a lightning blow to Elyria's stomach, driving the breath out of him and rendering him speechless, struggling to remain on his feet. With both hands gripped together he dealt another crushing blow to the back of his neck. He dropped, unconscious, to the dew forming on the roadside.

Chip fell too, but young Calvin quickly helped him sit upright, picked up the ropes that had bound him and tied Elyria, hand and foot. Chip watched in wonder and appreciation while this was done wondering what would now happen to him.

"Sorry, I didn't recognize you immediately. I didn't until you came into the firelight. You're one of Ben Shell's men aren't you?"

Chip exhaled a soft sigh, which in reality was, "Thank you Lord." He nodded a vigorous yes to Calvin's question wondering still how he knew the man. For a brief moment he thought of the prophetic biblical words, "The Lord works in mysterious ways."

"I don't recall your name, but you are Mr. Shell's harness maker, right? I saw you in the leather room when my father, Phinius Forman, came to pick up some belled reins you made. That was last year. I'm Calvin Forman, his son. I wish you could talk, tell me why you're here and what is going on." He could see the tears running down Chip's cheeks, "Are you hurting, in pain? Can you talk at all?"

Holding up his hands and shaking his head, Chip stopped the questioning. He wondered if he should show the hidden purchase papers or his free man papers. He decided to pantomime the situation. To Calvin's questions he nodded in reply then with little gestures revealed everything that happened. It wasn't long before Calvin knew the whole story and decided what he would do next.

Being free of his bonds the strength returned to Chip's limbs and he had no trouble helping load Elyria into the wagon. Tying his horse to the tailgate, Calvin stepped aside to recover the nearly empty bottle of whiskey then climbed up to sit next to Chip on the wagon seat. They headed toward the harbor along the still dark but starlit road. As the pink blush of dawn settled on the clouds they reined in the wagon. Calvin took the bottle and forced its contents down Elyria's willing throat. Now they waited for the fiery ball to carve the horizon into heaven and earth.

Still very early, the wagon turned off the road and rolled onto the planks of the dock. Calvin went in to the harbor master's office.

Chip sat quietly watching the sleeping Elyria. The two men returned to the wagon and they looked at the man in the back. Chip produced the purchase papers, getting directions to the hides just beyond a ship making ready to depart the harbor. Pulling the wagon up to the gangplank, Calvin and the harbormaster boarded the ship.

"Captain I've a new crew member for you," said the officer.

"I'm in need of a good man. Where is he?"

"Sleeping off a night of celebration in that wagon there," a finger directed his attention to the wagon.

"You know I don't take no man without his wanting to ship out. Is he able to sign his mark to the crew list?"

Calvin spoke up, " I can assure you he told both of us," a piercing whistle came from his mouth and Chip turned to acknowledge the prearranged signal, waving both arms over his head, "have heard him say many times that he wished to go to sea."

"Can he make his mark?" the captain repeated.

"Perhaps, with a bit of help. I mean he is sleeping. I'll try to get him to answer you, if you will grant me permission to have him brought aboard."

"Be quick, the tide is right to depart."

Calvin hastened down the gangplank to assist Chip in his struggle to get Elyria to walk aboard. The two men held the stooped figure upright.

"Elyria. Elyria Oats, here's the trip you wanted. You ready to sign on for sea duty?" Calvin asked.

A moan.

"Good. Here's the quill." He couldn't grip the feather tightly enough and it slid from his grasp. "Let me help." Taking Elyria's hand firmly in his, Calvin placed an X on the crew list.

"He's your man Captain," said the harbormaster as he and Calvin began walking back down the gangplank. "Thank you and safe voyage."

The harbormaster accepted Chip's purchase offer and soon the wagon was loaded and moving off the dock. Calvin accompanied Chip back to the Shell place to help explain the situation. They had worried for nights about the disappearance of Chip and the wagon and were making arrangements to search for both now.

Chip was dismayed that he could only listen as the story was told. It had been an adventure that he would like to tell about. Being a free man, Chip's request to remain at the Shell place was granted with pleasure. He was able to retell the tale of his adventures many times over the years to the children and the adults that came to the Shell farm to visit or buy leather goods made by him.

Wedding Vow

Millie, looking down at Arthur her husband of fifty-two years, and murmuring to herself said, "...in sickness and health, 'til death do us part." She felt a twinge seeing him wired to monitors with tubes pumping air into him while a bladder bag dripped liquid as it hung from the lower bar of the slightly raised bed. Millie felt a bit light-headed from the walk from her room down the hall, pushing her walker gently before her. Sitting next to Artie, she clasped his hand in hers, closed her eyes and took a deep breath.

"That's how I found them," the nurse said to the doctor. "The both of them holding hands."

Looking for a Job

The director of internal work programs hung up the phone and stepping into the outer office asked his secretary, "Have we hired any recent applicants that can speak and read English?"

"I don't know Mr. Edwards. I'll check immediately."

"Yes, and see if there are any applicants coming in today too."

"Yes sir." Margaret Taylor was out from her desk and heading for the employment section of the company before Mr. Edwards reentered his office. Sitting in the employment office were two women, one gazing at the ceiling the other intently scanning a copy of Readers Digest. Mrs. Taylor made a quick choice and approaching the reader asked, "Are you reading that article?" The question was in English and the answer would let her know if she was satisfying Mr. Edward's request.

The woman looking up to Margaret closed the book. "Yes, I'm reading."

"Are you looking for a job, Miss..., Mrs...?"

"I am Miss Lois Sanchez. Yes, that is why I am here, for a job."

Mrs. Taylor told the employment clerk she was taking the woman to see Mr. Edwards and sent up the employment form to his office. In the outer office Margaret asked the woman to sit, then knocking at the inner office door, entered and told Mr. Edwards about Miss Sanchez. Mr. Edwards went at once to the woman. Margaret stood back in the doorway very pleased with herself.

"Miss Sanchez, I'm told you understand English and that you can also read English. Is that true?"

"Si. I understand English. I also read English, but I don't understand the words."

"Weren't you reading a book downstairs?"

"Yes, yes. I was reading the book pictures, but not understanding the English words."

Margaret slumped in the doorway and said nothing.

A Traffic Problem

Harry held the homemade sign up to the approaching car with one hand and tugged at his jacket collar with the other. The chilly breeze and the falling rain were making hitchhiking on Old Route 66 difficult this morning. On the road since 7ish, he'd spent the entire time walking without an offer of a ride. In seconds the car zipped by but another was right behind it so Harry's sign continued to dangle from his outstretched hand.

This car, too, left Harry standing on the roadside. Muttering several profanities under his breath, he saw the tail lights brighten as the car came to a halt and eased onto the shoulder. Harry didn't run to the halted car but he quick stepped and hopped in as the door swung open.

The driver was a man about 50, 55, heavyset and while wearing a suit, wore no tie. Smiling, he pointed to the sign in Harry's hand then to himself, vigorously nodding his head. Harry must have given him a bemused look of wonder. The driver's fingers did a little dance, then one finger went to his ear and he shook his head, "No." Harry understood at once. The driver was deaf. Harry mouthed the word "deaf" and the driver proceeding to move his car back onto the road nodded, "Yes."

The ride was quiet, not the usual give and take of most of his rides. Harry's sign, "Vegas" in large block letters must be the destination of the driver too. Harry, touching the man's sleeve for attention, put his hands together and pressing them to his cheek closed his eyes for a moment. It's amazing how the human mind perceives things, but his little mime got a "yes" nod from the deaf man. Harry could sleep if he wished. So Harry, shifting in the seat, conked out.

If there was a siren, the sleeping Harry hadn't heard it. He did feel the cool air pouring into the car as the window opened. Next to the car stood a highway patrolman. The driver's fingers were moving rapidly even as the officer looked at the man's license. Looking over to Harry he asked, "Do you speak?"

"Yes I do officer. I was asleep and don't understand what has happened. Can you tell me?"

"Good, you talk. Can you talk to," he gazed at the driver's license in his hand, "Mr. Temple?"

"I wish I could, it's been a very quiet trip for me. I just found out his name from you. He is driving to Vegas and I'm riding with him."

"Oh, boy. I'm in a bit of a dilemma here." Shaking his head and scratching his chin the officer returned the license to Mr. Temple. "This guy was weaving all over the road. I thought he was drunk or drinking. Has he been?"

"Not this morning" Harry looked at his watch, "Not since about nine o'clock."

"Well something is wrong here. I can't let him drive."

"I'll lose my ride."

"Tough on you." A smile cracked his face in half. "Will he let you drive?"

"Let's see." Harry plucked Temple's sleeve again. Pointing to him, Harry mimed the sleep sign he used before. Temple pointed to himself and nodded, "Yes." Now came the tricky part. Pointing to himself, Harry mimed driving then he pointed at the driver and moved his pointing finger to his seat and mimed sleep again. Another nod of "Yes."

"Well, Officer, he'll let me drive."

"Looks like you're still going to Vegas. That's a good four or five hours down the road." Back in the patrol car the kindhearted officer smiled and waved as Harry drove onto the pavement and waved too. Out of sight of the officer, Harry decided to cut the driving time down to four hours. His heavy foot pressing down on the gas increased his speed.

"Oh, damn," Harry uttered as the red and blue lights atop the car behind him began reflecting on everything shiny inside the car. The wail of the siren sought the attention of the driver in front of it. That was the car Harry was driving. Mr. Temple snoozed on totally unaware of the pending situation. Harry rolled down the window as the grim faced patrolman stepped to the side of the car. Without much money, he realized he was a dead duck. He seriously doubted if Mr. Temple would save his butt.

"May I see your driver's license and owner's card please?"

"Cripes, does every cop say the same thing to every driver he stops?" His mind was racing. Mr. Temple stirred, remaining asleep. The idea struck with the power of a thunderbolt. Harry began to sign. He knew nothing of signing but his fingers and hands jiggled excitedly all over. The officer stared in wonder.

Harry did some pointing and finger exercises. He smiled coyly and gave the man a bewildered look.

The Arizona State Highway Patrolman shook his head and shoved his pen back into his jacket pocket. He moved a little more toward the head of the parked car so the driver could see him. He signed flawlessly to Harry, "Please show me your driver's license."

I was told a story like this by my sign language teacher, in ASL.

Could Silence be a Sin

The banshee screeching of the 7:17 express's wheels changed to loud clattering, whining, whirring alarms as it left the tracks. Screaming, cursing, yelling vocalization followed the inexorable sudden silence as the commuter train stopped its forward motion. The switching device had frozen in the below zero weather causing the work bound passengers and the steel frame carrying them to leave the tracks, fusing blood and metal together in a dying mess.

Chicago policemen controlled the onlookers while firemen, hustling like ants harvesting picnic crumbs, carried the live bodies to waiting ambulances and deposited the dead in rows. Railroad workers and assorted volunteers wearing identifying arm bands clambered through broken windows and ripped open panels to hand out the lucky living and the unlucky dying. By noon the entire nation was aware and watching man's valiant attempt to help one another.

Father John Grant moved along a row of the dead giving his final blessing and begging Almighty God to forgive them. He moved quickly, disturbing no one, his breath clouding his vision at times. He felt something pulling from under his foot as he prayed. Frightened, he turned to see a man's hand slipping away. The voice issuing from the body, thought dead, was very weak.

"Forgive me..." came the familiar whisper of a Catholic confessing.

"Yes, yes," came the amazing reply. The priest bent low saying, "I'll get help."

"I'm dying, listen. I killed Sarah Cooper. Cut her throat and stole..."

Father Grant looked into the closing eyes and realized death had ended this confession, but he was still warm. Maybe there was a chance for him. "Help! Help! He's still alive. Help!"

A stretcher bore the man to a waiting ambulance and Father Grant continued his work among the dead, touching each body in hopes of saving another victim. Many hours later he headed back to his parish where, tired to exhaustion, he fell into his bed and slept. Hours later a visiting newspaper reporter informed him that the man he had rescued was alive in the Illinois Central Hospital. It was expected that he would live. Amazed by the news he decided that tomorrow he would visit the man he now knew as Chester Lavender.

In the morning, enjoying his second piece of toast, Father Grant began choking. The coffee and partially chewed toast gushed from his mouth across the table, splattering the two priests that shared the rectory. Both came to his assistance, pounding him on the back until he pulled away from their violent thrashing.

Still gasping, "I'm OK. My toast caught in my throat." Righting his chair and making an attempt to help clean up the mess he created, Father Grant, scooping up the newspaper, retreated toward his bedroom. "I'm going to change my shirt. I'm through eating. And I am sorry for, for, you know," waggling his forefinger at the table, "this."

In the solitude of his room he flopped into the old Lay Z Boy, his fumbling fingers finally finding the article that nearly caused his strangulation at the breakfast table.

Landlady Killer to Die, the heading of a news item read. A jury had found Samuel Frost guilty of the murder of Sarah Cooper. He had cut her throat when she interrupted him burglarizing her rooms. Mr. Frost, one of three roomers in Miss Cooper's home, was the man who called the police to report her death. He claims he awoke from his sleep about 2 p.m., his usual time, to work the 4 to 12 shift. Leaving, he noticed Miss Cooper's door ajar. Knocking on the door caused it to move slightly and he saw the old woman on the floor. Going in to assist her he knelt down in the blood seeping from under her head. According to his statement to the police, he got up and used her telephone to call the police. While waiting for them, her body lurched and thinking he could help her, he went and turned her over. This caused the spray of blood the police found on him when they arrived a few minutes later as he stood at her kitchen sink washing his hands and face. The top drawer of the hutch in Miss Cooper's was partially open, some papers spewed upon the floor, but no money was found. Mr. Frost was taken into custody.

According to evidence given at his trial, Samuel Frost had been the only person in the house since early morning, the other two roomers having left together and ridden the same bus to their job at the Speigel's Warehouse. Frost could give no proof of his story. Upon further investigation it was found that while in the army he had been accused of participating in a violent attack upon a citizen. Charges were dropped when it was proven that he was on KP duty when the attack occurred.

At this time Judge Walter Thorn has set April 5th as the execution date. Mr. Frost's attorney has filed an appeal.

Father Grant proceeded to change and left the rectory at once. Riding the bus to the hospital his thoughts rotating over and over in his head, he failed to notice the hospital stop and got off at Midway. Walking back, his head tucked deep into his shoulders to avoid the biting effects of the lake wind, he visualized the discussion he'd have with the man he had saved. Would Chester Lavender confess to the murder and set Mr. Frost free? Why had he stayed silent during the trial? Did he think he wouldn't be convicted in the first place? Question after question rocked around in his head. Finally he walked up the hospital steps asking himself one big question. What could he do if Lavender stayed silent? After all, he knew the killer because of his confession and a priest is bound to silence.

Lavender did not recognize the priest; however, he suspected when he saw the clerical collar as the man removed his overcoat. He immediately turned his head away, gazing at the wintry scene across the street. The priest eased a chair between the window and bed, knowing in his heart he would have difficulty with an obstinate man. He was right.

Alone with this man, Father Grant spoke sotto voce as he introduced himself, explaining the circumstances of their first meeting. Chester acknowledged the meeting admitting some vagueness to all the facts. When the confession was mentioned, steely eyes glared at the priest and with lips pursed tightly he gave a negative nod of his head.

"You can't talk about that."

"I can't talk about it outside the confessional, true. I want you to talk about it."

"You're nuts, Father."

"You will allow another man to die for what you did?"

"Sure. I don't know this Frost guy I don't owe him nothing." Flat on his back, Lavender, smiling all the while, asked Father Grant, "I'd be a dope, wouldn't I, if I spoke up now?"

"You would be saving a man's life. That is a marvelous thing to do." Pausing with his finger rubbing his chin, "There is no greater love than to give your life for another."

"Nice speech. Let him give his life for me." With a wide grin Lavender turned away, "Go bother someone else. I have nothing to say to you or anybody."

Father Grant tried to visit Lavender several times in the hospital, but he had requested no visitors. When he left the hospital he moved out of state leaving no forwarding address. Somehow Father Grant was able to intercede on Frost's behalf and a judge spoke to the governor which resulted in a commutation of the death sentence to life in prison. Never did Father Grant find the courage to face Mr. Frost, for he feared he might not have the strength to remain silent.

The Viet Nam War came and went, man walked on the moon's dusty surface, the Berlin Wall crumbled, a president left the White House in disgrace and Frost remained behind the bars and walls of the Joliet Prison. Father Grant moved from parish to parish as was the practice of the diocese. Chester Lavender, unbeknownst to the priest, resided in the Federal prison in Atlanta. Today, 36 years after that fateful train wreck, a small item on the obit page indicated that Chester Lavender had suffered a heart attack in his cell and died in the prison hospital.

Father Grant rubbed his hand over the few gray hairs of his balding head. He had an appointment with the Cardinal, though he knew what the answer would be, he had to find out what he could do for Mr. Frost. He took a cab to Holy Name Cathedral to hear mass, then attend his meeting. The cab driver summoned the policeman standing on the church steps. His passenger was dead in the back seat. For one man the waiting was over, for another the waiting continued.

Learning

Walton had been told many times, at home and at school with his class, don't take a big bite if you're not sure you'll like it. But it looked so delicious and the others might take it before he sampled it. Pushing the others aside, he took a huge bite. Walton was served as the main entree at the fish dinner that night.

Taxi Ride

Dooley could feel the fatigue settling in as he slid into the taxi. It had been a long day and without much sleep last night he was now exhausted. He'd get to bed as soon as he got home.

The police arrived at the single car accident with the paramedics. The briefest medical exam, feeling for the carotid artery pulse, told the paramedic Dooley was a D.O.A. The probable cause of the accident, the driver falling asleep at the wheel.

Losing Faith

The little bell above the door began bouncing like a drunken chicken as two women stepped into the slight coolness of the tiny resale shop. They had seen, from their apartment across the street, the shop owner dragging a large and obviously heavy box off the vendor's wagon and into the shop. Rushing right over, even helping remove items from the box, would give them first choice, well second after the shopkeeper made her choices.

It was early August 1902. The city street, where once the more affluent local women stopped before shop windows to appraise displays, had changed. The windows hid the shop interiors from view with layers of weathered grime. Today's locals knew the green grocer's because of the boxes of fruit and vegetables stacked before it. The meat market was known by the malodorous smells frequently emanating from behind, as well as in front of, the screened entrances. The other shops also proclaimed their specialties by sounds and odors. The loud music and laughter came from three bars. The barbershop's red and white pole mutely beckoned customers. On the corner, for all to see, hung three greenish balls where the more desperate citizens surrendered their prized possessions for a short term loan, 'til payday. Madam Lucy, owner of the resale shop, did nothing to summon customers. They came in when they needed something for themselves or family members.

"Got some new things, Lucy?"

Lucy, arms tugging at the sides of the box now caught on the edge of a counter, looked up at the questioner. "Ah. Yes I do Mrs. Flint. Yes, I do." Swiping the back of her forearm across her brow and sucking in some dusty warm air she proclaimed, "As ya can see, it is not yet on display." She looked over at the younger girl, "Ain't been in much Birdy."

"Been working this summer," replied the girl. "Workin' takes up lottsa time."

"Birdy and I would be glad to assist you in hopes we might be given a chance to make some selections before some of the other neighborhood ladies stopped in."

"First selection, not at a lower price than I decide? I'll consider it," Lucy said.

Iris Flint gave Birdy a shove, "Give Madam Lucy some help movin' that box down the aisle."

The budding teenager stumbled forward and began lifting the caught corner of the box saying not a word. Together the three women arrived at a clear area surrounded by some makeshift garment racks. The cord holding the box together was cut, the contents removed and piled up to view.

"Cold weather goods," shrugged Lucy, "Clean forgot it was mostly that."

"Cripes," Birdy whined. "I don't even wanna touch or try on this stuff today."

"You will if you find something you want," her mother wheezed, bending down to retrieve a jacket from the floor.

"Lucy." The shout came from the doorway. "Lucy, I came over to see if you're needing help. Saw the box delivered a while ago and thought, as your friend, you'd like some help."

"Oh, Mary, Mary. Don't you always know just when I need you."

"Mary Conway, you can see Birdy and I are already helping here," Iris Flint called out. "Don't you be sucking up to Lucy and hoping to grab something nice for yourself."

"Listen to who's talking. Wouldn't be you and Birdy was only helping without looking for yourselves?"

Taking the jacket her mother had picked up from the floor Birdy moved toward a mirror behind Lucy, swinging it over her shoulder. "Look at this mom, beautiful and fits like, like, like..." Birdy slid silently to the dusty floor, clutching the jacket to her tiny bosom.

"Holy Mother!" Mary Conway yelled.

Unable to see from her side of the box, Iris, unsure of what was happening sang out, "Birdy, Birdy. Birdy, girl what's wrong?" Concerned, she tried to ease her bulk onto her toes, then began to clamber onto the box with partial success. She tumbled off the box knocking her head and lay dazed upon the floor too.

Meanwhile, Lucy went to Birdy, knelt beside her and stroked her head rousing the girl. Mary Conway joined them as Birdy began a piteous moan. As her eyes opened, she searched the room and the faces before her before tightly clutching Mary's arm.

"Momma! Momma. They have killed me." She spoke in a husky tone instantly recognized by Mary Conway. The voice was the voice of her daughter, Faith, the child who disappeared nearly two years ago. Hand to her mouth in fright and awe, Mary screamed, rose to her feet and bolted from the store, Birdy pleading for her to come back.

Several women, already wending their way to the resale shop, watched Mary climb the stairs across the street. She was blubbering incoherently and pulling away from people attempting to help her.

Returning to her flat, Mary seized Faith's portrait from the little shrine created the day after she disappeared and collapsed with it onto her unmade bed. The young lady in the picture wore a jacket identical to the one in the shop. Mary Conway could make no sense of the past few minutes, the strangeness befuddling logic.

Back in the store, excited and confused neighbors were curious to see the girl they knew as Birdy Flint proclaiming, in a voice many seemed to think belonged to Faith Conway, that she had been murdered. As a tabloid, nothing was in place. Birdy, in body, told Lucy to stay away from her in the voice of Faith. Iris Flint, now on her feet, didn't understand why the girl standing in front of her, Birdy, her very own daughter, rejected her attempts to comfort her. Beat officer Mick Delaney, drawn to the shop by the increasing growth of the crowd of people in and out of the place, gently shoving bodies aside, finally arrived before the primary characters.

Seconds later at his loud insistence the women began retreating from the shop. Lucy, her mind in a fog, somehow urged, pushed and shoved friends and do-gooders wishing to stay and help, out the front door. In clusters of threes and fours they stood and discussed what they knew and speculated and enlarged upon what they didn't know. Something strange was happening on their street, very strange.

Questioning the three women was impossible Officer Delaney concluded after listening to some of their comments. The only practical thing to do was accomplished when the paddy wagon arrived to take Birdy/Faith to the hospital. Iris Flint reluctantly agreed to ride with Lucy and Mary to the hospital, where police Sergeants Cooper and Moss met them. Resisting the staff's efforts, Birdy was sedated and taken to a padded room where a nurse was assigned to watch her.

All the original questions and answers produced at the meeting that morning were destroyed years later. So the reader must sift through memories of those people recalling the incidents, and stories that circulated about the strange goings on after the police tried to solve a missing person case.

Two days later Mary and Iris, after discussing Birdy/Faith's behavior in the shop and in the hospital, agreed that the girl would live with the person she chose. It wasn't an easy decision, but something had to be done. Faith stayed with Mary Conway and this created all sorts of unbelievable occurrences. She knew where everything was or belonged in the apartment, made recipes known only to Faith and Mary, knew family secrets, family members and strange facts about them, located a lost earring, and wrote down many things forgotten by relatives long ago. It was mystifying to all. However, many times each day she repeated her original accusation of Lucy, "Momma! Momma! They have killed me."

In her shop, Lucy refused to listen to questions, asking the questioner to leave at once, or locked the door refusing to open it. Police Sergeant Moss was assigned to investigate the case. He had accompanied Kyle Hart in the original case of Faith Conway's disappearance and didn't agree when the file was set aside as that of a runaway girl. Now he went over and over the written records. Nothing notable stood out.

Mary Conway watching from the corner window, which projected out over the sidewalk above the Green Isle Saloon, saw her daughter crossing the street, heading for school. Kate Ahern, Lucy's wild daughter exited the shop and ran after Faith.

Kate, for the record, said she caught up to Faith and the two continued to school. The school records for that day were incomplete because the regular teacher was absent and an assigned teacher, Ivory Martin, arrived late. She also taught the first class with difficulty due to the missing classbook of the regular teacher. She had taken it home to work on lessons. She also failed to account for the names or number of pupils in the room. Various inquiries of students and teachers yielded vague memories of Faith being in class that day. No person could swear to her being there except Kate. "We come in together and she went down her hallway and I went into my room just around the corner."

Perplexed by what he read, which told him nothing, Sergeant Moss returned to Lucy's shop. Perhaps Kate might remember something, anything which could aid this investigation. Early in the morning Lucy answered the silhouette repeatedly knocking on the dirty glass door, but only after hollering she was closed did the silhouette respond with a bellowing, "Open the door, Lucy. It's Sergeant Moss, I got questions needing answers."

Dressed in a tattered night dress, hair bunched atop her head like a tilted haystack and arms akimbo, "Couldn't wait 'til ..." Her belch fouled the doorway air with sour alcoholic vapor. "OK. What questions need more answers? I told Delaney everything."

"I read his report. I need to question Kate."

Lucy's eyes squeezed shut tighter than her lips. Her hands went to her hair and pulled violently destroying the haystack. A tiny trickle of blood stained her lower lip as she spoke in a quaver. "Moss, you forgetting the trolley accident," she pointed over his shoulder, "right there." Hand shaking and tears flowing down the ample cheeks she continued, "Forgetting my Kate died, cut up then cooked by them crackling over head wires. Nine people died there and I never knew one was my Kate 'til I saw her lifted onto the curb."

Moss blanched, his face paled and his voice softened. "Sorry Lucy. I did forget. Sorry." He shook his head and stepped back. "I had something else on my mind. Sorry."

"Well now Kate ain't here to answer no questions, but why you wanna be questioning her?"

"I have read and read and read again the report of Faith Conway's disappearance. I can't make anything of it. So, I was thinking maybe Kate might have missed something and might remember it now." Moss pausing to look around the untidy shop had the most bewildered look come over his face and he began stammering, "It's this Birdy talking like Faith Conway, knowing all about the Conways. Then she's always repeating, 'They killed me,' and I'm thinking, who is they?"

"Don't like that talk. No need for it." Lucy's hands plucking at a tilted pile of folded blouses shook slightly. "What bothers me most is how it sounds, ya know, that sortta low husky voice. Us women that heard it think it's Faith speaking. Scary as hell it is, Sergeant Moss. Real creepy."

"The Conway woman, Mary, says she started talking when she put on a coat."

"Nope. Was a jacket."

"You still have it? Can I see it?"

"You can see its ashes in the ash barrel out back. Burned it."

Lucy's pronouncement brought a frown to the policeman's brow. "Guess it frightened you to have it here, huh?"

"Yes. Now look, Sergeant Moss, I ain't had my coffee or nothing. I got things to do too, so can we stop talking? Ain't getting us nowhere."

"One favor. Can I bring the girl here?"

"What?" Why?"

"I want see what she does. It may tell us something. I mean, she might be faking this voice thing. Everything. Whatta ya say?"

"If I say yes, do I have to be here?" Lucy kept shaking her head no, even as she agreed to allow Moss to bring her in. "You bring her over here now. I will leave the door open but I'm leaving soon as I go up and dress. I will stay away exactly one hour. You lock the door when you leave. One hour."

Sergeant Moss behaved a bit differently after that day, never revealing what happened in the shop. He retired from the police force in 1929 with comfortable investments in various banks and business firms. Two years later he gassed himself to death. He wasn't the only victim of the stock market crash and the depression that spread over the country in the early 1930s. Among the meager belongings he left behind was a cryptic diary. It went to his son, who, after skimming through it, thought it nonsense and tossed it into the coal burning stove that heated his two room flat.

Had he kept the diary it would have read:

Aug.18, 1902

I didn't fill out my report on my experiment into the goings-on at Lucy's shop today. They will run me off the force or send me to the nut house. I'll say this much it scared the shit out of me. I never believed in ghosts or spooks or things like that. I do now. I didn't see them but they were talking all the time we were in the shop. If I hadn't locked the door after Birdy and I were inside I think I'd still be running. Mrs. Conway didn't want the girl to go but the girl wanted to and we went. I told her to do whatever she wanted and tell me anything she wanted while we're in the store. I would not talk to her but if she asked for help I would do something. She started walking to the back and went over and touched her hand along the wall near the stairs. Just standing there she began talking, not in that husky voice. Someone else answered her in a husky voice. Birdy asked why she killed Faith and the other voice said she was already dead. I listened real hard, but I can say I was shaking. Birdy was speaking for Faith. It went like this:

Birdy - When we started walking I told you go slow. I got my monthly and hurt. Then you said you did too and took your mom's medicine to reduce the pain.

Voice - I told you you could have a sip of mine. Just a sip, 'cause I only had a little.

Birdy - I already had some morphine from my mother, she uses it. But God I hurt.

Voice -You wanted some of mine, so we went behind the shop fence so no one noticed us.

Birdy - I guess I took too much of yours.

Voice - You looked sick right away.

Birdy - I was sick right then.

Voice - Uh huh you went down on your face I called you and you looked at me and didn't talk. You died. You died.

Birdy - No I didn't die I was sick. My body wouldn't move. I couldn't talk.

Voice - I know you did. You stopped breathing. I was so scared. I wet myself I was so scared.

Birdy - But I was alive I saw you run and leave me.

Voice - I ran to get my mom.

Birdy - I was crying for you, I called you.

Voice - No you didn't. I didn't hear you call. I came back with my mom. She hit me, hard, for giving you the opium. It was hers and I stole it. God she was mad.

Birdy - You both came back. She came and knelt down to look into my eyes and I hollered for her to pick me up.

Voice - No she said you were dead. She said we were in trouble and the police were going to catch us and we would go to jail.

Birdy - But I was alive when she picked me up I could feel her breathing and her heart pumping. I told her to get my mom but she carried me downstairs.

Voice - I know and I asked her why and she said to bury you cause you were dead.

Birdy - I was afraid, real scared. I hollered and hollered when she started pushing me into that little old ash box you had next to the furnace. The pushing hurt.

Voice - Mom kept telling me never to say a word about burying you. She told me to go to school and not say anything.

Birdy - I hurt but I could hear you talking then your mother pushed me harder and my throat was crushed and I passed out. I died when you came to see me after school.

Voice - I'm sorry. For a long time I cried every night then one evening getting ready to get off the trolley the wires broke. A fire started and people pushed me into the glass and I got cut bad so I was bleeding and then a wire fell on me and the electricity went through me.

Birdy - Why are you talking to me now?

Voice - This is the first time you come into the shop since I died that's why.

Birdy - Is it, really? Sorry I didn't want to come in and cry.

Voice - Well I got another reason. Faith is always crying down there. Somehow she got my spirit to come into the shop after I got killed outside. Now she keeps me here. Her crushed throat don't let her talk above a whisper and she whispers and cries all the time.

Birdy -So?

Voice - So I thought, when I saw you come in, I could be you and show you where she's buried and you dig her up and bury her. She'd be gone and not whispering and I could go too.

Birdy -How? And wouldn't your mom get in trouble? You know, finding a dead girl?

Voice - Maybe. We got to do something to make them look downstairs in the old ash bin.

Birdy - How?

The talking stopped and Birdy turned to me. She started walking and fainted. I opened the door, took her out and set her against the light post and went back and locked the door. She was waking, but didn't talk so I took her home and went home myself. That night Lucy's shop caught fire and burned down. The old lady died in the fire. Some months later the wrecking company knocked over a block of cement in the basement. They found bones and I was sent back with Delaney to see what it was all about. A ring on her finger identified Faith. We could find no one to explain how or why she got there, just that she had died. Her mother buried her. I wrote dead on the Faith Conway folder and filed it.

I met Birdy a few times before I was transferred to a different district. I heard talk about her being a "bit tetched" but never noticed any difference in her. I heard several stories about her; she joined a convent but didn't stay, she married and moved to Chicago and that she died young in an asylum. I often wondered if these things happened because of her part in her ghostly encounter.

I want people to know this story but want no part of it myself. Maybe after I'm dead someone will find it and then everyone will understand some of my actions and behavior over the years. God forgive me for what I am going to do. N.D. Moss badge #2486

Parable

A wise and far-sighted farmer sent his only son into the vast reaches of the world to seek knowledge and find new plants for food and medicine. Roaming the many countries he became worldly-wise but used little common sense. He squandered his father's money by listening to the advice of foolish friends. He married without his father's blessing.

Presently he was without money and his wife and the fools had abandoned him.

Having nothing, he decided to go home when he chanced upon a field of wild plants and recalled the reason his father had sent him out into the world. He stripped the field of its seeds. Lying about their source and value, he gave the seeds to his father who praised his son then with great pomp and promise he planted the seeds.

Soon the flourishing new plants overran the fertile fields growing so fast the workers could not save the crops already planted. Before, they were controlled in the cold ground of their native land. But all of his efforts to control the new plants were abandoned and he gave orders that they be consumed by fire. The farmer spent all of his money trying to save his fields, but, ridiculed and reduced to selling most of his land, the father finally sent his son into the world again, with nothing.

In God We Trust

"You're damn right I know he's your brother. He got you into the organization when he talked to me." Benito "Buns" Gomez wheezed as he spoke, "And now I find out he's been talking to the cops, not the city cops but the government cops. Not good Ortega, not good for me, for you or for him. Kill him."

Lowering his head and shaking it back and forth, Ortega hesitated at the order. "Boss, I'll do anything for you. I ask you now, if my brother is talking to the government cops isn't it too late to hit him?"

"Never. If he talks once, he talks again. He's got to be stopped. Take him out."

"One more question. Can't Raul do it?"

"No, and don't make me angry by not thinking." Buns raised his ham-like hand in a threatening pose, then lowering it said, "Raul is my brother. If he goes to your brother right away he will be on guard 'cause he knows I know he's been talking."

Opening the door Ortega called back, "OK, I'm going." In a half whisper to himself, "Stupid, stupid brother. Damn."

Buns spent the afternoon watching the Marlins win another game before heading for the spa. Refreshed and relaxed he reached for the remote and clicked off the news program. Leaning back into the warm water of the whirlpool spa he smacked his lips. *"Well, that's the end of the blabbermouth. Ortega mustta got him as..."* The chimes of the doorbell broke into his thoughts. He listened as Raul answered the door. The familiar voice prompted, "I'm in the whirlpool Ortega, come on in."

"Got some chop suey to snack on later. I'll put it in the fridge. OK?"

"Yeah sure. Raul, you put it in there. Ortega, you come in here."

"He's already putting it in the fridge," Raul yelled back.

The long sad face and red eyes told Buns more than the TV news announcer had. They had found Vincento in his car shot in the head and were now asking the public for help in catching the killer. Robbery was suspected since his wallet was missing. Buns knew who the killer was as the newsman reported it. Ortega's face told the story, he had killed his brother.

Buns said, "Hand me a towel," as he stepped out of the water. Rubbing his face he continued speaking in a muffled growl, "I know it couldn'ta been easy. But I want you to know how much I appreciate it. You know the place in Cuba?"

Ortega nodded yes.

"You go there for a while. Rest, relax, jump a coupla dames and visit the casinos. Don't come back for a few days."

"The cops will wanna see me about my brother."

"Naw. I'm gonna have Raul fly you down there right now. They come looking for you and you been down there for several days." Taking his robe off the hook and slipping his arm into it he started for the other room. "We got a story for you already." He sat on the edge of a cushioned chair, "Raul, you got a suitcase for Ortega in the car?"

"Ready. We can go as soon as I call the airport."

"I'll call. Bye Ortega. You mean a lot to me." Buns patted the man on the back as they walked toward the door. "Don't stew about it. And be careful with them girls."

Exactly one hour later Raul picked up the cell phone Ortega had been talking on from the cabin floor while at the same time easing the small plane 180 degrees toward the distant twinkling lights of Miami. "Sorry Buns," he said, continuing the conversation that Ortega had begun a few moments ago. "Ortega stepped out to feed the sharks. He's doing that right now." Shoving the phone out the little window, Raul let it fall into the dark water of the Caribbean Sea far below. The door, recently opened to allow Ortega to depart, clicked shut as the plane leveled off for its return to the small airport.

"Cripes Buns," Raul remarked getting into the car with his brother. "Why'd we get rid of Ortega too? He done real good for us, well for you."

Driving onto Tamiami Trail, Buns pointed toward a couple reeling along the curb. "There's tomorrow's buyers." He honked and waved as he passed the drugged pair before answering Raul. "I couldn't trust the guy no more. I mean, would you trust someone that would kill his own brother?"

"No, don't think I could. Sorta like them brothers in the bible."

"Yeah, or on money, In God We Trust. You gotta trust Him. Him, no one else. So we're rid of them. Tomorrow call that kid, ahhh, you know."

"Tomaso?"

"No, no. Let me think," For the next few minutes muted street sounds were the only thing heard in the car. Buns pulled into a lower level parking space. They got out and headed for the elevator, still silent. As he opened the door he shouted, "Duncan. That's the guy, Duncan. Call him."

"Oh. OK."

"I'm hungry. Want some of that chop suey?" Buns asked dropping his jacket on the sofa while walking into the kitchen.

The morning newscast said the police were unable to explain the explosion that rocked the building off the Tamiami Trail last night. The two bodies found in the ruined upper living area were identified as the Gomez brothers, Benito and Raul, often brought into headquarters for questioning concerning Miami's drug dealing. Lucky Ortega didn't stick around for a snack.

Writers Write

"Writers write."

Stan heard this in nearly every community college writing class, workshop, conference and seminar he attended. He loved to use, twist and play with words. He wanted to write and learn from different writing instructors, and each evaluated, corrected, made suggestions and encouraged his writing.

Eighteen years zipped by. Stan never sent stories to a publisher, magazine, newspaper or agent. Piled everywhere, his writings occupied most of his living space.

After Stan died typing another story, the landlord packed his belongings, then rented the flat. Heirless, Stan's writings went to a recycling center.

Long Q-T

Mrs. Barrows, tense as a well tuned drum, sat across from the doctor listening intently to every word he said. Many she didn't understand and she intended to ask what they meant and how it affected her daughter. Connie, her newly wed daughter, had fainted in the kitchen just before leaving for work. She had never fainted before and doing so now had her asking herself all kinds of questions.

"No. Mrs. Wood is not pregnant. Her test was negative."

"I asked her about eating and she said she had breakfast."

"Mrs. Barrows," the doctor countered, "You're sure she has never fainted before? Shouldn't her husband be here to answer my questions?"

"Not to my knowledge. Never. I don't know why her husband isn't here."

"You know this is just the ER. I am new to your country, learning American medicine and I'm not her regular doctor. Earlier you both mentioned Dr. Storm as your family doctor. That's the Dr. Storm here at this hospital isn't it?"

"Dr. Frank Storm. Yes."

"I am suggesting you have him set up some cardiac tests for your daughter. Actually she should make the appointment."

"I'll see that she does."

A knock on the door and Tony Wood, visibly out of breath, entered the consultation room. "Hi Mom. She OK?" A gasp, "Damn traffic held me up."

Quick introductions and repeated information quickly ended the consultation. The ER doctor released Connie, who called Dr. Storm's office from the hospital and requested an appointment for the cardiac tests. In three days, after the results came in, husband and wife along with Dr. Storm and a cardiac specialist would review what the tests revealed.

Thursday, February 5, 2006, the Woods couple found out they had a problem. Not an impossible problem but one that would dictate how they would live every day of their lives for the rest of their lives.

During the introduction they didn't even catch the specialist's last name. Doctor somebody. She explained the critical factor in Connie's condition. She explained with words, diagrams, repeating one phrase so often it sounded like a mantra. "Long Q-T."

It drove Tony and Connie nuts. The explanation would not fit into their heads. So again, with sublime patience and simplicity the doctor hung the diagrams and test results on the wall behind her.

She sighed and looking intently at the young couple said, "Does it make sense now?"

"It does," Tony replied. The rhythm of the heartbeat gets out of sync and the heart gets screwed up and doesn't send the blood to the right place in her body so she faints. However, I don't understand how it could happen to Connie."

"Tony," Connie admonished, "the doctor said it happens. Accept it. It happened to me. To us."

"Long Q-T, it's nothing but a heartbeat."

"A heartbeat. A killer, well, a potential killer. But it doesn't have to be," the doctor said for the umpteenth time. "If you are careful, you'll live."

On her own, Connie arrived at the conclusion that they had to make some adjustments to their plans. Definitely no children. For the price she opted not to have her uterus removed, they would have to be very careful using the pill and condoms. Tony didn't like that. She set up an emergency contact program and took a class in emergency steps in case she fainted or felt faint again. She gave up her job and the exercise program she used at the health club. The exercises or the canceling of them made her feel like a hot summer road-kill flattened on the highway. That is, she felt lifeless. Tony didn't admit it out loud, but he felt the same way.

It wasn't long before Connie suggested they have children, not adopted but theirs. She showed him an article on surrogacy. His sperm in her egg implanted in another woman to carry and when born returned to them. Who? They didn't have a clue. They went to the library and read up on it, but didn't feel right about asking anyone they knew.

Victoria Carpenter wandered into the picture when she served Tony his order of espresso in the office building a new client occupied. While she took his lunch order, she bumped the table hard enough to upset the water glass. The resulting flood cascaded onto the table soaking the book he had set there. The waitress picked it up to wipe it off and noticed Surrogacy on the cover. It prompted a question.

"Do people really do that?"

"Do what?" Tony asked, unaware that the girl was referring to the topic on the book cover.

"Have other people have their babies." Victoria smiled, blushed and went on, "I just read about this," pointing to the word Surrogacy on the cover, "in some magazine. Do people pay people to do that? Carry a baby for nine months?"

"Yeah, some people pay. Other people get friends to do it, or get a relative, like a sister. I read where one woman carried her daughter's baby."

"I bet I could do that, get paid for having some woman's baby. It would be better than working here for damn near nothing."

Tony gave her an odd look and said, "Yeah. Look I need to eat and get back to work." He ordered, ate and left. That night he mentioned the conversation to Connie. And they agreed he should go back and ask the girl if she was serious. In the morning Tony begged off, asking Connie to talk to the girl. Victoria didn't work that day, so nothing happened. When the two of them finally met Victoria, she agreed to talk with them after her shift. The discussion came down to money and the cost was a year's tuition at the local college. The doctor ran some tests and agreed that Victoria would make a fine surrogate mother. The lawyers stepped in and contracts were signed. The baby would arrive in April.

Victoria violated the contract almost at once. Discussing her condition with Tony frequently, which was whenever he came in to order lunch. They were not to be in contact to avoid becoming too friendly with the surrogate mother. However, comments were made and not told to Connie, about movements, morning sickness, ad infinitum. Tony met her leaving work one day, she was sick, so he drove her home. He took her up to her flat. Tony always considered himself a ladies man and used this opportunity to hit on Victoria and the inevitable occurred. They agreed to a little mutual loving. Then he began stopping over and nature took its course. It was their baby. Connie was unwanted in their family.

Tony recalled the doctor saying exercise could kill, sudden shock could kill, bad news could kill, oh so many things could stop Connie's heart. He didn't want to hurt Connie by asking for a divorce. He suggested removing her to Victoria after one of their romps in the bedroom.

Victoria didn't relish the idea of killing Connie, but when Tony explained how he planned to do it, she had no objections. He would come into the room unseen, unexpected and yell while standing right behind her. He'd holler something sweet and tender, and then if it hadn't killed her she couldn't accuse him of anything. He would not meet Victoria tomorrow, instead he would go home and he didn't plan on telling Connie he was coming. He'd surprise her, even bringing flowers, for the anniversary of the first dinner she ever fixed for him.

Mrs. Barrows was befuddled by the description of the scene the police had found at the house. She had called the police when she couldn't reach Connie, stating she was afraid her daughter's heart might have acted up. The police arrived before Mrs. Barrows. Finding the bodies in the kitchen, they kept Mrs. Barrows in the front room and tried to explain what they found.

In the kitchen, the TV was giving the mid-day news and Connie was standing at the sink peeling potatoes for potato pancakes preparing the same meal they had the first time they dined together, which was followed by lovemaking. So quietly Tony approached her, so loud his, "These are for you," pushing the bouquet around to her face. Connie jumped and spun around. The knife dug into Tony's chest, tearing the flesh between the ribs, ripping open the pumping heart. Both of them lost the color in their cheeks and both slid downward onto the tile floor. As a matter of fact Connie's mother was right. Both of them had heart trouble.

With This Ring

Taking the small black box from his pocket again, Toby went over the words he wanted to say, again. Looking around he saw everything was ready for the big moment. The restaurant owner, Toby's Uncle Mike, saw him looking, pointed to the clock and hunching up his shoulders, palms up, indicated she was late. Toby nodded in agreement then turned to watch the approaching streetcar. She should be on it.

Paula worked at Sherwin Willams Paint Factory just off 115th Street. She could take either the Illinois Central suburban train or the Cottage Grove streetcar home after work, usually it was the streetcar. That was fortunate for Toby, because one day, rushing to get off in the rain she knocked him down. Gallantly Toby took the blame and invited her into Uncle Mike's to try and dry off. He enjoyed her company and began watching for her to get off the streetcar. A few meetings, some coffee and a little talk gave Toby some encouragement and he asked her to the movies.

Opening the box and looking at the small stone clasped in the thin gold band, Toby reviewed some of the little differences he and Paula had in the last month or so. Oh, he knew they were unimportant and his proposal would wipe them away, but a twinge of doubt existed in his mind, or was it jealousy, or stupidity or pig-headedness? He didn't know, didn't even want to think about it and drove the memory out of his head. He put the box away and stood to watch the streetcar unloading its passengers. She wasn't there.

"Worried?" asked Mike now standing beside his nephew and staring out the window.

"No, not worried. I was getting concerned, then I just thought, remembered, it's payday. She often stops at the currency exchange to cash her check. She doesn't know anything special is going on here, so she's in no rush to get here."

"Good thinking boy. No sense worrying about the unknown." Mike gave Toby a firm, friendly pat on the back and turned to an entering customer. "Table or booth?"

Cashing her checks caused one of their spats. Toby told her not to carry the money around without him to protect her. She went to Carl Krupp. He worked in her office and frequently rode the same streetcar with Paula. Toby had seen him help her disembark then get back aboard to continue his trip. Jealousy burned inside him and flared up when Paula mentioned Carl's attentiveness. It returned to rile Toby further when Paula told him she and Carl meet at a church social event.

As the next streetcar rolled to a stop, Toby spotted three employees from the paint factory. It's easy if you know a fact or two about making paint. These guys worked in dry color and, even after showering, their temple hair showed the color. All the protective clothing and masks they wore didn't stop their hair from collecting the colored airborne particles. Toby hurried out to ask about Paula.

He came back in subdued, his face pale and his eyes filled with tears and slouched down in his chair.

Pulling out the other chair, Uncle Mike sat and stared at Toby. "Something bad happen?"

"Bad for me, good for Paula I guess. Those guys just told me Paula and Carl took the South Shore train to Indiana. They were eloping."

Flora

Mathias "Matt" Silverman tapped *Save* into the computer, and watched the little green dot flashing as the translated document took its place in the memory. Months of patiently piecing together the tiny bits of ancient parchment were now complete. He was ready for the final images to be photographed. Walking to the wall cabinet he withdrew a bottle of scotch and two glasses.

"Honey, come on in, it's finished," he said, as he poured two drinks.

"Time for a toast?" Pat Silverman asked, stepping into the oven-like atmosphere of the room. "It's so hot in here, Matt. How do you stand it?"

"Acclimation my dear, acclimation." Handing her a glass, they gazed at the finished puzzle on the table. "A toast. A toast to Silvinius, writer of antiquity, scribe of fairytales."

"Silvinius."

Their glasses rose, clinked at an angle and shattered. That quickly, blood spurted from Matt's thumb and he twisted in surprise, dropping the remainder of the vessel onto the computer and the parchment puzzle. A bright electronic flash and a small wisp of smoke shut down the computer. Splashing across the puzzle without moving the pieces, blood quickly darkened the parchment. Astonished by things happening with such speed, both stood momentarily turned to stone.

This occurred nine months ago. Since then, Pat and Matt had written down every word they could remember of Silvinius' story. Both agreed, since the toasting accident destroyed everything, his story deserved to be told. It was finished, edited, proofread and hand carried to the publisher. Each held a copy of an unknown, 'til now, a mythical Roman fairy tale. Pat read,

"The Smell of Onion, by Silvinius. Great title," she said with a smile at Matt.

"It is."

She continued, "Angered at being awakened late again, Zeus raged at the dumpy little cook. Flora, the goddess of flowers, had chosen the cook for him, while his regular cook rested in the mountains. This was her third day cooking and the third day his breakfast was late. And why was it late? The cook had fallen asleep and the meal had burned. But why you may ask did the cook fall asleep after a night's sleep? Well, she didn't sleep. She stayed up all night thinking about and preparing the god's breakfast. Once she started cooking she relaxed and fell asleep until the heat of the burning breakfast woke her.

"Flora, I know you wish to please me and I know you picked a very good cook for me, but she is burning my breakfast and waking me late. Can you get another, more awake cook?"

"I will talk to her. Later today we will find a way for you to awaken and have a wonderful breakfast." Smiling she asked, "One more day? OK?"

"Momma," the bee-sized elf whispered into Flora's ear from her perch on an earring. "We have no time today for you to talk to cook. Today is the day we give each plant that flowers its aroma. Remember?"

"Oh, Scent," Flora said to her only child, born so small when the goddess had had a momentary maternal thought, "You're right. I have forgotten."

"Perhaps the wind, Zephyr, can help us," the tiny one suggested.

"Perhaps. I'll ask."

Zephyr agreed to help. Flora created an aroma and gave it to Scent. Zephyr then swiftly carried Scent and the aroma to a selected plant. Some plants still influenced by the cold season, had to be awakened. This slowed them down and the day was ending without Flora speaking to the cook. Very soon Flora would be turning in for the night. It had been a busy day for everyone.

The heat of the day warmed Zeus and he called for Zephyr to come and cool him. Zephyr came quickly, tumbling Scent about with his speed. She fell from the wind's grasp landing with a thud on the back of Zeus's neck. He, thinking some bothersome insect had come to dine on him, swatted the intruder. Scent was squashed, killed by the god's mighty blow. Zephyr stopped blowing, the lack of a breeze told all on Mt. Olympus something had happened. Zeus sent Zephyr to tell Flora of the accident.

Zephyr carried a saddened Flora to a very sorry Zeus. He held out his hand, returning the tiny Scent to her mother.

"If you can think of something I may do to keep Scent with us, tell me," the god said.

"I will try," replied the crying mother, clutching Scent to her cheek.

Zephyr carried them home. All night Flora wept and tried to think of a way for Scent to return to her. As Eos began her daily routine of arousing Apollo to drive his chariot across the sky, the cook began breakfast. Now Flora remembered she needed to talk to cook. At the same time an idea came to her. She pulled an onion from the earth, a plant not yet ready to flower and not visited by Scent. Flora wrapped her child in the folds of the onion. Then without telling the cook she added the onion to the cooking breakfast.

Feeling the heat, Scent strained to free herself. The effort allowed her to break free and fill the room with the aroma she still carried. Cook, pleased with the unfamiliar aroma couldn't sleep but moved about each corner of the room filling it with the aroma. The finished breakfast was presented to Zeus and he too liked the aroma. When Flora told him what she had done, Zeus approved. Scent would remain in the onion to be remembered whenever an onion is opened.

Wagon Train West

"No, Tom. No."

"I've made up my mind and we are going to Oregon." Tom
spoke not loudly or tersely but in his usual firm voice.

"But Tom, you had us sell everything for the fare here. We
came here to Marengo to live with people we know. You had Mr.
Rogers buy the land for our house and farm. Now you say we're
moving on." Tears flowed freely down Elizabeth's ample cheeks
until they dropped off her chin and darkened the dusty soil beneath
her feet. "Why Tom? Please tell me why. We have friends here, we
know no one in the Oregon Territory. Do we?"

"Woman, I said we are going on to Oregon. I will tell you
why, but you need not know, because I've already discussed selling
our land here for a profit, $80 dollars to be exact." A pleasant smile
stole across his face, a sob accompanied her reddening eyes and
wet cheeks. Patting the back of the horsehair chair Tom Ware said,

"Sit here and listen to why we are moving on to Oregon. I think you'll be pleased when you hear what I heard last night."

"Riding into Chicago with Anson was the most fortuitous thing that ever could have happened to us. While he went to the Palmer House to deliver his butter and cheese order, I overheard a man telling a group standing on the corner about Oregon. I heard him telling that crowd how beautiful the Willmette Valley is, of the mountains, the rich soil, and the teeming schools of fish swimming in the river. He reminded everyone of the Preemption Bill Congress passed; giving free land to those that cleared it, built a house on it and farmed it. Liz that land is free, think of the money we'll be saving," Tom droned on.

Slouching into the back of the chair she began to hear the entire story, from his decision to move from Vermont, right up to this moment. Often her mind drifted back over the past several months. She had been told many things about their move and so many didn't happen or changed as they happened. What would happen now? Bedtime found Liz remembering the pronouncement her husband made last March. She fell asleep recalling it.

"Liz, I just stopped at the Packer house and told Martin and Doris we are moving at the end of the month."

"Huh? You did what?" Liz questioned as she lifted and turned her head from the tub of scalding water where she was washing her daughter's dress. "Moving?"

"We are moving. We talked about it before."

"Tom, we talked about many things. We decide things together. When did we decide to move? Where?" Patting her wet red hands on her apron, "Can't we talk?" Liz asked, taking up the apron corner and dabbing at her eyes.

"Sure. We can talk every day we're traveling."

That was the end of the discussion, if Liz had anything more to say, any objection, to make it would be futile. She and the children, Beau, 3 years old and Violet, just 15 months, had cried at the loss of their friends and family when they left Vermont. During the ship's journey to New York mal de mer,

seasickness, masked the red teary eyes and lack of appetite. The Erie Canal
segment of their trip provided time to walk and enjoy some of the country's
beauty. The sailing vessel on the lakes, from Buffalo to Chicago, didn't create
the same sickness the ocean leg had. Tom bought a small wagon just after
landing, loaded up the children and Liz and headed for Marengo at once. The
entire trip took only twenty-eight days. Four days later they left for St. Louis in
the small wagon carrying essentials for the road. Everything else they would
need they could get in St. Louis. It was a restless night.

And everything they needed in St Louis cost more, much more.
Tom asked about and found canvas for a tent to house them. On
the third day they had a roof flapping over their heads and blankets
to roll up in for the night. He unloaded lumber at river's edge all day
and came into the tent that night with an iron stove on his back. Liz
cried with happiness and sent the children out for wood scraps
where the men were building sturdy wagons for the Oregon journey.
They had fresh bread and hog jowls with beans and coffee. Hot
food for the first time in days.

By the end of their first week, hard work sapped their energy,
but talk, talk and more talk with other families planning to move on
to Oregon helped shape their future. Some travelers planned to
leave the group they had joined at a place near Independence Rock
and head to California. Often dead tired at the end of the day, the
women had to get the children to bed, take care of themselves,
start the bread to rising for morning, mend torn clothing, wash and
pray while the men sat up and talked of their dreams. One night
Tom heard a man say he was from New Bedford, a fellow New
Englander. After meeting him, Tom couldn't wait to bring the two
families together.

The two women were both twenty two years old, each with
two children the same ages and both, they soon confided, expecting
another child. The friendship caused both women to seek each
other's company often, so often that Tom bought up the space, and
the few possessions not destroyed, of a hapless family whose tent

had burned down. This put Liz and Ann Slate two tents apart. Now they shared chores and child watching and plenty of just wonderful lady talk. Both women helped Connie Peal give birth to a little girl and both helped lay to rest mother and child twelve days later because both were so weak from the prolonged delivery. Tad Peal disappeared leaving his two-year-old son in the tent. The women discovered him sobbing, dirty and hungry. Titus Beach, already with four children, but well off, took the child home and Bess took him as her own.

All winter the construction of wagons went on. Big heavy hard wood wagons to carry everything a family would need on the trek and at the new homestead. Nothing was cheap and anyone hearing of a family backing out due to death or running out of money was Johnny on the spot to purchase anything for sale. Some such sales caused bad feelings, but most gave the buyer an edge on the future.

"Thomas Ware, why buy a crib? We'll be in Oregon before the baby comes. Take it back."

"Woman you have no sense. The babe will not be held all night. You'll get a good night's sleep."

"No Tom, we have no room for it. The dry goods, household things and food for the trip are more important. Take it back."

"They left earlier. If you don't want it, I'll get someone else to take it for the same price." Struggling with the tent flap, he broke the support rope and brought a section of their tent down on his head. The welt and bloody cut caused their neighbors to catch an earful of Vermont profanity.

"It's time for a meeting." The children ran through the tent area and the work area shouting out the message Hans Melon wanted delivered. Hans Melon, burly blacksmith from Racine Wisconsin, had been picked as the group leader. He didn't back away from some river ruffians demanding food from families tenting near him, but sent them flying toward the muddy river banks. He didn't need to save the one that screamed for help in the dark water, but reached out and yanked him ashore. The group saw in him a leader and without dissent elected him. It was a good choice, for he settled many problems quickly and fairly.

He also gave each family a list of things needed for the trip and information for the wagon construction. If asked why he replied, "I have listened to those who came back because they didn't have these things or enough of them. The list started with the wagon. Use hard wood, for it must carry nearly twenty five thousand pounds. Why so much? Because you will need to have tar to seal the seams, grease to put on the axles, and wheels to replace a broken one. And it must float to navigate the streams and rivers. Also drill cloth to cover your belongs from rain or snow.

You need to eat. Yes there is game out there, but which of you has the time to spend hunting for your daily substances? Who? Bring what I suggest for the well-being of your families. You need flour, bacon, rice, coffee, sugar, salt, saleratus (baking soda), dried fruit, beans, rice, vinegar, tallow and some choices of your own. Also, and these are just as important, pots and pans, a coffeepot, frying pan, kettle, knives, tin plates and coffee cups. Don't forget powder, lead shot, extra rifles, tools to make repairs, and your livestock. And if you have it fine, but if not, get some money, maybe a thousand dollars for the ferryman, to replace broken parts, and replace lame or dead animals. I strongly suggest as many as eight oxen to pull such a load and to rest a few each day. And you will need rope, not miles of the stuff but plenty. The rivers are wide and some hills steep. Get rope."

Now this tower of strength as he climbed up onto a wagon hollered out, "Does anyone know the day?" He looked over the crowd around him. He was standing on the box seat of an unfinished wagon, smiling at everyone, and he laughed as everyone did when a child called out, "Today."

Several responses, all different, didn't settle the mystery. "I'm calling it Thursday. Reason, we need a day of Christian worship soon 'cause we are ready to began the journey of our lives. In four days we will join right here for worship. We will then start our travel. All men with wagons ready will assume their assigned spot. Do not move your wagon until I call out your place in the train. Moving before that will only create problems and we don't need problems. If there be any wagon unready when your spot is called, yell out and we will get the next wagon moving. Those that miss the call can catch up. If not join another group. We can not wait longer."

The men of ready wagons moved about, giving some help to others. Two men, soon joined by two more, began playing light music.

"Listen to that music," Ann called over to Liz as she walked toward their tent.

"Lovely. I'd dance but this," clutching her belly, "is a mite heavy."

A guffaw from Ann, "Mine too." Falling into each other's arms they laughed. "What's your spot?"

"Nine. Yours?"

"Fourteen. Close enough that we can walk together."

"Ain't ladylike but holler and I'll hear you. Or send Beau up."

"The children. I'd forgotten them for a moment. I must talk to Tom about a sleeping place for them in the wagon. For us too."

"Liz, I better leave, we need some planning time too."

The singing softened and stopped with an "Amen". Stepping up on a wagon tongue, Hans Melon stood tall and statue-like before the group. "May Almighty God guide and protect us, His servants, to the Promised Land. Oregon here we come. The crowd roared its approval, drowning out the first few called numbers. Waving his hands for silence, Hans called, "One."

"Castle, moving out," called the driver.

"Two."

"Bower, moving out," accompanied the crack of a whip.

"Three," Hans boomed out. He progressed down the list. Ten responded with, "Ain't hitched up yet. Go by me."

Within the half hour twenty of the twenty-two wagons in the group were creaking out of St. Louis west to a new life. The number ten wagon came into the first night camp after many families had bedded down. He informed Hans that number eighteen would not be joining them. Soon after starting their wagon had sunk into the spring mud and broken an axle. They had already joined another group planning to leave in ten days.

Within the first week the women were complaining that their bodies were unaccustomed to this heavy work. In the second week Ann bent over in pain, "Oh Liz, I'm so sore, every muscle in my body is screaming. I'm going crazy just trying to do daily things."

"Guess we both are." Rubbing her back as she rose from next to the smoldering campfire, Liz teetered for a moment. "If only I could sit and rest awhile."

"That's it, sit and rest. It's go, go, go. I get up, start the fire and get some coffee going." Turning her head, she watched hundreds of buffalo feeding and moving away from the wagons. "I never suspected so many of those big brutes traveling with us. Ruth's husband said they'll supply food for us and the Indians for hundreds of years."

"Well I'm thankful they at least give us these," picking up a dry piece of their manure and prodding it into the tiny campfire. "They have their own odor 'til you cook over them, then," sniffing her sleeve, "you smell like them."

"Is that what we smell like?"

"We do. And Tom said we'll smell this way all the way to Oregon."

"Mom," Beau called. "Violet says she's sick. Her head is real hot."

"Go see, Liz. I'll keep breakfast going. The men plan to eat here anyway."

"Violet, Honey, can you stick your head out here?" Liz asked as she came around the back of the wagon. "I can't get up there 'cause of my belly."

The head in the open flap of the tent didn't even look like her Violet. The sun was turning it to brown leather, the soot of the fires blackened the edges and irritated the white of the eyeballs a fiery red, and her lovely hair was snarled and limp. There was a button missing from the dress that created an opening showing the contrast in her actual body color, pink. But it showed the concerned mother even more. Red splotches dotted her daughter's chest.

"Stay right there Sweetie. You're going to be all right. Stay there. OK?"

"OK, momma," and she slipped back and down, out of sight.

Moving quickly wasn't easy doing the carrying a baby waddle, but Liz moved as quickly as she could back to the fire and Ann. The urgency in her step gave Ann some concern and she stepped toward her friend and companion.

"Sick, or something serious?"

"I need to find Tom. And don't you go near Violet. Please."

"Tom is there," pointing toward the herd livestock. "The men are moving the oxen to each wagon. We'll be moving in an hour I think." Ann reached out to give Liz a reassuring pat on her arm. "See him?"

She must have because she started in his direction. "Tom. Tom."

He looked at Liz moving along the edge of the line of wagons. Even after weeks of moving the oxen into their positions, the animals resisted and he strained to move the half-ton beast into the yoke. Unable to stop, he waited for Liz to join him, cinching the straps of the harness automatically.

"Problem Liz?"

"Yes Thomas, a big one I think."

He knew there was a problem the moment he heard Liz call him Thomas, not Tom. "You're OK?"

"Yes." Moving close to him, she whispered into his ear, "I think Violet has the measles." Pulling her head back she looked into his red, tired eyes questioning what he had just heard and nodded yes.

"Oh God," he muttered under his breath. "For sure? Want me to check, I've lived through them."

"Check if you wish, but I lived through them too." The deep concern for the others in their party furrowed her forehead. "What can we do?"

Tom went straight to Hans, told him the problem and with mutual agreement had his oxen drag the Ware wagon out of line isolating them from the group. Good-byes were called out as the wagons started out in hopes of beating the disease. Liz sat on the ground. Tom, holding her close, consoled her the best he could. Ann called her good-byes loudly adding, "You'll catch up, I know you will. I will see you at Ft. Kearney, we'll be making some repairs and…" tears cut her short then she hollered, "God Bless you all." The wind carried the creaking of the heavy wagons and the morning haze away from them, leaving the sun to warm their bodies, for the chill of isolation couldn't be warmed.

Walking with Tom at the head of the oxen each day, Liz tallied the cairns and burial mounds they passed. Some newer graves had names she knew from their party, but some had no name on the grave. She prayed for each and begged God pass over her close friends. Being alone on the vast open landscape stunned them. It was so immense, so flat, so windy, so empty of everything but grass and buffalo. And looking ahead at any given time it continued to be the same. If it wasn't for the ruts gouged into the soil by the heavy wagons wheels they would be lost. Eleven days and 38 new graves later they saw campfires far ahead of them. Liz urged Tom. Tom in turn urged the oxen and wanting news and friendship urged them to travel further that day. The sun had fallen below the flat horizon hours before their wagon stopped behind the last wagon in line. As tired as she was Liz tramped beyond the stop, heading straight for Ann's wagon and some woman-to-woman talk. And to find out how many and whose graves of the 38 new ones, were from their group.

Freda Malone, bending over the evening meal campfire, called out. "Liz, so good to see you. Your Violet OK?"

"Both the children are OK they're back with Tom. I'm looking for Ann Slate's wagon. "Know how far up it is?"

"Liz. Their wagon ain't with us. Castles, Burns and the Slates joined two other wagons that claimed they knew a short cut. Ann Slate and her baby died of the measles pox and her husband buried them and said staying with us and maybe you catching up would be unbearable. So he took off with the kids." Freda enclosed Liz in her arms as she started to drop to the ground. "Easy, Love, easy."

"Dead, she's dead and the baby? Dear God, I can never let my Violet think her sickness caused such a thing."

"Didn't. The Bowers let their youngest play with a child in a different camp. When Mrs. Bower saw the scabs she right quick took the boy back to their wagon.

He didn't catch them, but for sure started them in our train.

"Oh dear. The time I've spent praying ..." Liz grimaced as the unborn kicked her insides. "Near time. I'd better get back to Tom. We should be reaching Ft. Kearney soon."

"Liz those dark outlines are Ft. Kearney," Freda said pointing into the darkness of a moonless night. "If the baby is coming, do you want me to take you in? They should have a doctor to help you."

"I must tell Tom."

Freda spun around and reaching under the wagon, gave a sharp poke with her boot to a bundled blanket. "Thaddeus, up boy. I need you to fetch your father at the Hyde wagon. Tell him I'm helping birth a baby for Mrs. Ware and need him here. Then go to the last wagon and tell Tom Ware his wife is in the fort. Tell him to come and you stay with his young."

Tugging at the worn leather boots, the boy started running with a hop and another hop before the boots covered his feet.

"Want your arm on my shoulder while we walk?"

"Might get there faster if I did."

In the morning Tom Ware brought Beau and Violet to Freda as directed by her. They ate boiled apples and mush with hot coffee, then went in to see Anne Ware, their new sister. That evening the family was back together. Violet was holding her sister while Liz directed Beau to turn the ham slice the fort officer had given the new baby because his wife was also named Anne.

Hans Melon called his shrunken group, there were eight wagons now. Two brothers had signed on to drive two different wagons for two widows with their children in exchange for meals and clean sewn clothing left by their husbands. Louis Page, newly discharged from the army also became part of the group, working for Hans Melon at any task needing to be done. Ten weeks after leaving the Mississippi River banks and they were not yet half way to Oregon, but they were still going there. Good-byes and tears, hugs and small items changing hands, the crack of the long whip over the heads of the oxen, and hope urged them along.

Four days later the wagons moved slowly through a snorting mass of undulating buffalo. The men walked between their oxen, disguising their presence, the children huddled in the wagons, staring over the box seat at the lumbering beasts. Hans directed each man to stay in position, moving only if a wagon had trouble. They were losing time but better time than a wagon or a life. After six hours the lead wagon edged out of the herd, followed by the others in short order. James Bonnet, one of two brothers that had joined the group just after leaving Ft. Kearney, asked Hans' permission to bring down two of the beasts for fresh meat. Camp was made and meat was shared.

"You can't catch me," screamed one of the boys darting between the Ware wagon, now fourth in line, and the following wagon.

Three boys pursued the screamer, turning sharply to avoid bumping the oxen. Their screams faded as they rushed back toward the last wagon.

"Beau! Beau! You watch what you're doing," Tom hollered as he recognized the blackened face of one of the boys. "Liz," he called back into the wagon where she sat nursing little Anne. "Those kids need to stay from between the wagons. I'm telling the other men tonight that we need to keep them off to the side."

"Think they'll listen?"

"For the boy's sake, they should."

The next day the boys were seen running further away and out of sight often. Come camp time Ezra Pool came asking about his boy. Beau said he had not seen young Pool since about noon. The other boys gave the same answer. The boy was gone. Sarah Pool insisted someone go back to look for him. Ezra cautioned that traveling in the dark would do no good. In the morning the father and Sam Bonnet, one of the brothers, started back looking for signs of the boy. Hans Melon kept the train moving, telling the two men they were expected back in three days.

When they returned without the boy, speculation was the Indians had taken him. Sarah had a marker made with James Pool carved on it and an arrow in the direction they were traveling. Perhaps the boy was lost and would find the marker and come along. Stoic Sarah admonished the boys all day as they chased each other or scooted away from the wagons to fetch dry buffalo chips for the evening fire.

Several weeks later the Snake River became their next barrier. The preceding two days were rainy and the river water swirling before them created hesitation and fear. James Bonnet volunteered to go upstream with his brother to attempt crossing. He would attach one end of a rope to a tree. Sam watched his brother clutching the saddle horn as the horse swam toward the other shore. Rider and horse were better than halfway across as the water swept them passed the waiting wagons. Loud cheers went skyward when they saw horse and rider make the far riverbank just before the bend would have taken them out of sight.

"James," hollered Hans Melon, "can you tie off your end of the rope to those willows behind you?"

James looked back at the trees. "I can. But it won't give much slack in the rope."

"Do it," Hans yelled. "Once it's secure we can get more rope across with some men. Then we can form a ferry out of one of the wagons. You ready?"

"Ready. We'll need help over here too."

"The first ferry will have the extra rope and some men." Hans asked for volunteers that could swim, even warning them of the dangers of the trip. Sam Bonnet and Louis, the discharged soldier stepped forward. "Best strip yourselves for the ride, no need for heavy wet clothing if something goes awry and you need to swim part of the way," Hans suggested.

Immediately the first two wagons began the tedious task of unloading. "It seems that every river we cross we're pulling everything out of the wagon and loading it back up. Never expected this extra labor," one of the women complained.

"Sometimes I'm tempted to forget a piece or two just to reduce the load," her companion answered.

"I thought that too, but I couldn't. We've brought it so far." Rubbing at her lower back she added, "There go the men. Being bare sure shows the dirt and grime on the arms and faces."

A roar of happy cheering went up as they waded up the bank. Hans and several men seized the rope and tied a pair of yoked oxen to it. "Start pulling boys," ordered Hans as he and the men urged the animals into the water. The animals snorted and struggled against the current, but the ropes held and soon the partially emptied wagons were being ferried across with helpers to reload them as they came over. Hard fast work and carrying bigger loads made the crossing go swiftly.

The setting sun lit the sky in glorious shades of pink which was turning a copper color when Hans untied the rope and waded into the water. "Water's cold fellas so pull me over quick." Hans didn't tie the rope around himself and midway across a floating branch ripped the rope out of his hands. His screams alerted everybody to his trouble. They watched his splashing struggle as the branch pushed him under the water, silencing his pleas for help. In moments the branch and Hans disappeared around the river bend. Nothing could be done. The accident happened so quickly. It was a solemn group bedding down that evening.

Sam Bonnet was elected leader the following morning and he started the wagons moving after brief prayers for Hans and safety for all on the rest of their journey. The following day some of the boys racing about the uneven landscape discovered an abandoned wagon, its contents strewn about. Three naked bodies had been unearthed from beneath a stone cairn and partly eaten by animals. They had heard that Indians often dug out the dead, taking the clothing for their own use and leaving the bodies unburied providing food for the wolves.

They left the bodies and the wagon as they found them. In this case it was not unchristian behavior; they even felt pity for the Indians. Still standing was a crude cross bearing one tar-smeared word, COLERAH. One of the great fears among the travelers, or for any group anywhere, was the swift killing disease cholera. Three days later, a small pole lodging was seen and the clothed, partially eaten bodies of four Indians lay close by. Again, it was left untouched.

The trail became more difficult, food supplies dwindled and the weather felt cooler as they plodded higher into the low hills and soon got their first close look at the mountains they had to cross. Of the eight wagons that moved out of Ft. Kearney three or four months ago, only three remained. Days, weeks, months, no one remembered time anymore. They worked all day, and rose in the morning to repeat the same routine. They bartered some shirts away to a family of Indians for some fresh fish and two small pumpkins. And they seemed to bury someone every day or so.

In April a group of Indians ventured into Ft. Hall to trade their furs and some pots, pans, knives, blankets and sundry items usually found packed into the wagons of those heading for the gold fields of California or Oregon. One brave wore a cross around his neck, another carried a mighty fine rifle but had no bullets, powder or shot. They were carefully questioned about these things and the fort officer accepted their story.

Over the broken country to the north they had found the ruins of a wagon which had fallen into a rugged rocky canyon and had became useless. The other two wagons held the bodies of some women and children. No man's body was found. They said the bodies were huddled together, arms wrapped around each other. The report made reached this conclusion. A party traveling to Oregon had become lost. Without food and perhaps buried in a snowstorm, the men decided they should try to go for help. They didn't make it and the family had starved or frozen to death, an unfortunate but true occurrence in the old west.

Discharged

Cpl. Amos Feathers, watching the doctor and several students work their way around the ward, mentally practiced his delivery and facial expressions for his request. *With a pleading weak smile and tearfully choking words, "Come on Doc, let me go home, just for a visit. A weekend. I only live 70 miles from here. I can take a cab there for God's sake. Please? A weekend?"* He went over it twice more before the little entourage finally stood at the foot of his bed.

Dr. Hardy Stone, his mother thought it cute when she named him, scanning the papers on the clipboard hanging from the bedstead, proceeded talking without looking up. "Amos, how do you feel?" He passed the clipboard to a student. "Going to ask me if you can go home today?"

"Fine. You know I'm going to ask." Amos felt the weakness in his facial muscles as he spoke his lines. He thought he saw a tear in a female student's eye. She's on my side he thought. "It's only 70 miles from here," a cough, "Just for the weekend?"

"Yes, Amos. Feeling that good are you?"

"Real good. No pain at all." The clipboard passed over his bed to another wannabe doctor. "I know I'm improving."

When the clipboard returned to Dr. Stone, he didn't hang it on the bed, instead he handed it to Amos' favorite nurse, saying something Amos couldn't hear. She looked at Amos with one of her warm smiles and walked off toward her cubicle with the clipboard.

The entourage turned to go with the doctor, stopping as he turned back to Amos. "There's no pain Amos, none at all," he said, shaking his head "Everything is arranged."

Amos couldn't speak. He knew the doctor was letting him go home. Watching the group leave, tears filled his eyes, *"I'm going home. Home."*

He heard the soft shuffling steps of the nurse returning to his bed. He grinned curiously when she stopped next to him. Tears were coursing down her cheeks as she covered his face with a clean, white sheet while singing softly, "Going home, going home…"

I am Perfect

Casey wanted to show Mr. Ruben just how good she really was. She convinced him to donate the company showroom for her wedding and reception. The caterer would prepare the food outside the building, one of the new windowless monstrosities, to prevent the cooking odors from permeating the offices. Her guests would park in the side parking area, with direct access to the security guarded entrance and elevator to the showroom. She wrote everything down and checked that all guests, even the minister, understood that timing was essential.

The day of the wedding, she received a phone call from her mother just after 11 o'clock. "Honey turn on channel 6 right now."

"Why?"

"Do it."

Channel 6 was showing a lovely painted scene of deep snow. The channel 6 weatherman's voice describing the scene was saying,

"This freak storm, dumping four inches of snow in an hour has stopped Atlanta in its tracks. Nothing can move and nothing is. Beautiful isn't it?"

Is It or Isn't It

"It is."

"It isn't."

"It is. Come to your senses my friend, this is not a copy. It is an original Rembrandt. Look at the strokes of the brush, the coloring, the composition and the signature. Everything on the canvas is screaming out from the canvas, original."

Bill Sands, art collector and recognized expert on the paintings of the Dutch masters, particularly Rembrandt, was once again defending his position as to the authenticity of The Guild Masters Daughters. This particular painting was discovered by the son of a Nazi officer when he attempted to sell a painting he knew his father had purchased from a dealer in 1948. It was The Guild Masters Daughters reputedly done by Rembrandt in his early years. Museums and art collectors laughed at the man saying he had been cheated, the painting was a forgery. He hung on to it, after all it was his and it was lovely to look at.

While cleaning the frame and wiping off the painting, Herr Kliest detected a color difference at the edge of the canvas previously hidden by the edge of the frame. Thrilled by the discovery, at least momentarily, that a more valuable painting might be hidden under the questionable Rembrandt, Herr Kliest took it to Herr Schone, a teacher he knew at the Berlin School of Fine Art. From there the two men proceeded to the Art Museum to request an opinion and possibly have some tests conducted. They would soon know if they had a painting of value.

Within days they returned to the Art Museum with high hopes to hear the results of the test. "Sorry gentlemen, our tests prove only that the paint is quite old. Nothing more," the senior lab technician reported.

"Old paint? How old would you guess?" asked Herr Kliest.

"Without guessing the laboratory consensus is," he referred to a notebook, "300 years."

"A painting covered by paint 300 years old and it's not valuable? To me, that is valuable. My father thought so and now so do I. I will not sell it."

Herr Schone shook his head sadly and placing his hand on Herr Kliest's shoulder said, "My friend, much as I want you to keep the painting, you know you must sell it. If you do not your house and the other things you treasure will be taken by the State to justify their tax claim."

A sigh, followed by a deeper sigh and the man's hands extended out from his sides and came down with an audible smack on his empty pockets. A single small tear pushed over the lower eyelid, but remained there, not heavy enough to fall. A lump formed in his throat almost blocking his words. "Damn. I know."

"Then don't dilly-dally about." He started for the door saying, "I must return to my classes. Call me tonight, we can have dinner and discuss this then. Bye."

Opening the door he bumped into a man entering. "Sorry," and continued down the hall.

Poking his head into the small conference room Philip Husemann, Museum Director asked, "Have we a valuable painting?"

Like a soldier before an officer, the man reporting snapped into a rigid stance, "No, Herr Director. Herr Kliest, owner of <u>The Guild Masters Daughters</u> thought he had discovered something beneath that painting. It seems from the laboratory tests that it is only some old paint."

"Hmmmm. Too bad Herr Kliest." The director pulling gently on his beard, looked to his employee then to the technician and at last settled his gaze on Herr Kliest. Pursing his hands together and smiling he inquired, "I understand you are in need of money. True?"

"True."

"Would you consider selling your painting to the museum? The price you must understand is for a painting of a questionable reputation."

"Herr Director, it is a Rembr...."

"Not proven," the director cut in. "Will you accept 80,000 guilders?"

"Herr Director, please. You know that is less than half the offer Rosen made just, what, five or six weeks ago. I will go to him and perhaps he might keep the original offer."

"No need to go to Rosen. Here, use the telephone and call him."

"You will accept what he says over the telephone?"

"You know I will. You, and everybody else, know I am an honest man and I cheat no one. Some of my detractors have told stories about me, lies." The director wore a hurt look. "Go ahead, call. Rosen knows the painting as well as I do and as well as most museum directors or art collectors do. Call."

Before Herr Kliest hung up the phone the price had gone up to 100,000 guilders beyond the price the director had first given. Somehow, some way the two men raised their bids until the unbelieving man sold his painting to the Museum for 180,000 guilders. He couldn't believe his good fortune.

The evening newspapers were short and black with ink, **ART DISCOVERY**.

An article said that the Art Museum had discovered, beneath the much maligned painting of Rembrandt's The Guild Masters Daughters, an original Rembrandt. The museum estimates the new discovery is worth several million guilders. When Philip Hausmann, the museum's director was asked if Herr Kliest would share in this discovery, the prompt answer was, "Not a guilder. The purchase was a fair and honest purchase."

That night in the museum's back office the director toasted the laboratory chief, "Your discovery of the Rembrandt under that dreadful forgery was most timely. Letting me know so I could outfox Kliest and Rosen is giving me a very good feeling. We're rich."

Herr Schone opened the front door and welcomed Herr Kliest into his house. They shook hands, beaming at the thrill of sticking it to the director. With time and patience the art teacher had painted the new Rembrandt where it could be discovered. When he left the Art Museum office he stepped into the phone booth and took the pre-arranged call pretending to be Rosen. So in the end we ask the question; is it or isn't it a forgery?

Brrrrrrrrr

Someone tipped Thurston Mallet at his office about his impending arrest and he ran. He embarrassed his friends, clients and family. Mallet, a city boy, wanted the luxuries of life and embezzled thousands of dollars in just a few years. If he could escape immediate arrest perhaps he could make a deal with the courts and not serve time. However, he did have a hidden Swiss bank account and could live in comfort in some foreign country.

The cabby thanked his fare for the generous tip and watched him enter the hanger of Executive Charter Airlines. Within the hour the Lear jet had the harried businessman looking down on the green treetops of Canada's vast wilderness. But minutes later the engine died and the plane skimmed across the small frozen lake and dug a trench into the shoreline. Thurston Mallet had several new problems.

Dressed in torn business clothing, with no broken bones or serious cuts, without food or water and with a dead pilot, he certainly had no idea of his location except the sun was over there, and Minneapolis was over there too. Mallet decided to walk toward the sun. He took the pilot's flight coat, his cigarettes and matches and started walking along the shoreline.

An hour later, cold and depressed he began collecting bits of wood for a fire.

Misfortune appeared at once. There were only three matches and cold fingers failed to light his meager kindling. Frustrated and freezing, he succumbed to despair and sat down and cried. The bitter cold overcame him quickly and death claimed him soon after. Mallet's stiff body slumped sideways falling against the log he sat upon which dislodged his glasses. Sunlight, focusing through the glasses, ignited the rotting dry wood of the old log a minute or two later.

Shooting up

Mike sat on the locker room bench as the other players headed out to the field. He carefully removed the hypodermic syringe and needle he had prepared earlier. He knew he'd need this fix before the game started. He gave himself the shot, replaced the needle in his bag and walked onto the field. He'd play well today, he thought, as the insulin began taking effect in his diabetic body.

Think, Then Act

Mark recognized the snake immediately, a diamondback rattler. It was coiled tightly under a shrub to avoid the heat of the sun. He knew there was danger and the snake reminded him with its ominous rattle. Being back about twice the length of the snake would be a safe distance for taking pictures.

Mark tumbled backward as the snake's fangs dug deeply into the back of his forearm. While squatting down and focusing his camera, the snake lunged at him. This shouldn't have happened. Mark had failed to consider how much more snake was coiled under its body. Also, he failed to consider that he was alone and quite a distance from help. Rest in peace Mark.

Tell the Truth

"You give us that meat pie or we will make your chickens dry and your pig die," the scruffy boy yelled.

"We done it to other folk that didn't do as we told them," Jockum, the eldest of the three ruffians, said.

"Get away you filthy gutter tramps. I'll have my husband crack your heads." Frau Lomax slammed the shutters and pegged them shut. "Otto! Otto! Gutter boys are threatening to curse our chickens and kill the pig. Go out and chase them away. Otto!"

A stout farmer, his skin darker than his farm soil and now angrier than a cat getting a bath, rushed through the door. Looking about he saw the three boys moving toward his pig sty and gave a whoop. They turned, and seeing the man rushing toward them immediately raised their arms their fingers rhythmically wiggling. Their voices were hollow and low, mumbling an incantation. Poor

Otto, heedless of the pitchfork left leaning against the well wall, stumbled over the errant tool.

"Stay down you old fool. Stay or I will turn your legs to stone."

Otto, a superstitious farmer of Bamberg, Germany in the year 1626, felt pain in his leg, injured when he tripped. The pain was caused by falling over the handle, but Otto already knew the boys had cursed him.

"Stop! You want the meat pie? Come back, I will give it to you and you will go away? Leave us alone, yes?"

The gravy burned their grubby little fingers and stung their tongues. Finishing it in hasty gulps, Jockum, sucking on each finger between words, said, "Don't forget to tell your friends that we can curse them too." Laughing and pushing, the three hoodlums strolled down the road chanting gibberish for the old man to hear.

It is strange that three young boys, Jockum Berger, age thirteen and the Isenthal brothers Franz, eleven and Pawl, age eight, would wander the countryside proclaiming themselves capable of casting spells upon people or animals, yet historical documents show it to be true. History also records what happened to these youthful possessors of satanic powers. These were the days of witch hunts and persecution of witches by torture. Having confessed, they were put on trial and soon followed suitable public punishment, usually a violent death.

That night the three boys slept under the stars, their stomachs almost full, their heads almost empty. They wore stolen clothing either too large or too small. Franz wore cloth shoes. Their breeches were held up with rope and pegs. Cleanliness came with the rains and their bodies stunk of filth and urine. Jock wore a scarf around his neck to cover an ulcerated carbuncle. His teeth, broken in fights, were snags of brown. Franz and Pawl had been driven from their home by families not willing to raise them. Jockum had been sold to a cooper that abused and beat him until he fled.

By chance, in the city of Bamberg, they passed a seller of apples on the street. They grabbed apples and ran in different directions thus avoiding pursuit. Jockum ran behind the church wall sheltering the firewood. Franz and Pawl, ducking behind the animal shed, were munching their purloined bounty when they saw a man seize Jockum. Dragging him along the street while pounding him with his fist, this man intended to gain some recognition for capturing a thief.

Franz, bolting from his hiding place, ran up to the man and delivered a kick to his groin. Screaming in pain and falling down he released Jockum. The boys ran, passing Pawl who quickly followed them. This time they ran until they reached a knoll from which they saw no pursuers. Now they laughed and introduced themselves. It was a quick and easy joining of company, as they had the same needs and desires.

Tramping in and around Bamberg that spring the three boys often sat around the square or near St. Martin's waiting for an opportunity to steal the food to live or something to wear or sell. They listened to the people visiting and shopping in the city talking of witches, and of reports of people being denounced as witches and their seizure by churchman or appointed officials and ultimately their trials. Also mentioned were stories of people being threatened or of having someone cast a spell on them, causing mischief, sickness, crippling or death. Once someone was accused other people often remembered something to add to the accusation.

On one of their sojourns out of the city they were following a farmer with several fine half grown geese, which they planned to steal. Jockum suddenly ran ahead and accosted the farmer.

"Best you give us a fat goose old man or I will tell my friend the devil of your unkindness and have him kill them tonight while you sleep."

"What's this? What do you mean I should give you a goose. Get," and he lashed out with his boot.

"Give me a goose or...or." Raising his hands in front of his face a grunting, Jockum circled about the stunned man.

Setting his cage down the old farmer began to counter gesture, to ward off Jockum's spell. Paying no heed to his cage he fended off the swaggering boy. Franz ran up behind them grabbing the cage unseen by the occupied man and ran to the woods nearby.

Jockum stopped his clumsy act as Franz cleared the rise. Bowing deeply he yelled, "Thank you my Master for punishing this selfish old fool." He ran a few steps and turning watched the bewildered man looking high and low for his cage of geese. "Careful I don't ask the Devil to give you horns," he shouted, running off to join his unseen accomplices.

That evening the three, having eaten all three geese, discussed the ease with which they accomplished their theft. It was decided that by threats they'd find life a bit easier, with fewer bruises and less pain, than when they had been caught stealing. They would try in the morning.

In the morning Pawl was deliberately caught stealing eggs by the woman of the house. Jockum came at once to his rescue. The woman was about to be cuckolded by a very clever trick. In his hand Jockum hid a toad caught earlier that morning. He startled the woman by jumping at her and grabbing the stolen egg from her hand. Pawl slipped from her grasp, moving to Jockum's side.

"Woman, you will feed us or by tonight I will cast a spell that will have all your chickens laying toads." He thrust forth the other hand holding the toad. "Well, feed us."

The confused woman saw only the toad not the switching of hands. She blessed herself repeatedly with the sign of the cross. Unable to speak, she motioned for the trio to sit. Bread, cheese and sausage were placed before them by their frightened hostess. She carefully moved about, never once taking her eyes off the group.

"Thank you, good woman. We are refreshed and will take our leave," Jockum said. "And for your prompt service I will not place a spell upon your flock. I will even return your egg," which he withdrew from some hidden pocket in his clothing. Extending the hand holding the egg he said, "Remember, some day we may return this way, or others of us may stop by. Don't wait for a spell to be cast, feed us, thank us and you will remain free of spells for the Devil protects those people who serve us."

With this kind of success the boys began enjoying life. They threatened and the simple folks produced. Not all peasants were intimidated by the clumsy act the boys performed. Often they were driven away by irate citizens, pelted with rocks or poked at with forks and other tools. Some times they would return that night and wring the necks of every chicken, drawing symbols on the walls with their blood. One night they stole a cow and left in its place a turtle. All night they walked until they sold the cow in the next village.

Spring changed to summer and the boys traveled the countryside moving from place to place, avoiding a place already visited. They had a bit of fear that talk among neighbors might catch up to them. The one time it did they were lucky to kick out and replace a shed board and escape before the growing mob beat or killed them. Jockum left his toad behind, hoping the simple folks would think they had escaped by changing their form. They would never know.

Their route was circuitous, bringing them back one morning to Bamberg, which they didn't notice until they walked into the square. Having grown some and wearing different clothing, they sat near the town well, watching the movements of the townsfolk. They were hungry and the smell of fresh bread from the bakery coaxed them into action.

Again Jockum took the lead. Entering the shop he asked, "Herr Baker, may I have a roll, please?"

"Sure, for a pfennig you get a roll."

"Do I look as if I have a coin, even a small coin?" Jockum held out his arms in the familiar gesture of having nothing and continued speaking, "I will have thousands of beetles eat your flour tonight if you don't do as I ask. I want not one but three rolls," pointing to the other two boys standing at the door, "One for each of us." The boys shook their heads and stepped in to join Jockum. A barrel shaped man happened to follow the boys in.

"Herr Kaufman, I think we have trapped, here, the three boys who cast the spells at Neff's farm, perhaps the same ones that caused Shulman's litter to die because the sow went dry. This one," a hand clamped down on Jockum's shoulder, "demands rolls for all three, but he has no coins."

Kaufman, the walking barrel, blocked the door yelling out to the citizens in the square, "Der Baker, has trapped the Witch boys. Come help tie them up and we'll take them to the cathedral. Be quick before they flee by becoming birds or dangerous animals."

Coiling their arms, the three boys began shouting, "Toads, frogs, snakes and eels, become you. Master Satan we appeal. Change them now so we may be gone. Change them with a spell they will always remember." They had practiced this chant walking the roads and sang it loudly. "Toads, frogs..." they repeated.

Some men, rushing to assist in the capturing of the Witch boys, halted their approach, however, others, seeing no demonic change, held the boys tight stuffing bread into their mouths so they couldn't speak. Ropes were found to gag and bind them and a few blows were applied to stop their wiggling efforts to escape. In a short time word spread throughout Bamberg that the Witch boys were caught. Several messengers were sent to people that were threatened by them, telling them to hurry in and identify them.

Pawl in his quest for glory told the assembled crowd of the threats they made to gain their daily bread by praying to the Devil. He told of Jockum turning things into toads and frogs, he swore he saw this happen. He saw Franz and Jockum dance before a fire and send it into farm sheds when the owners chased them off with sticks and stones. Many leading questions were answered by bragging and embellishment. He was condemning all of them without realizing his stories would be denied by the older two.

Their demeanor brought jeers from the crowd, condemnation from the clergy and sentencing by the lord mayor. "Death. These three shall die by burning at the stake." Men gathered faggots of wood, piling them close and high to three separate stakes placed in the square. Several jars of oil and a barrel of pitch were poured over the wood. Ready hands tied the screaming Jockum first.

"I was lying! I did it as a trick," he yelled. "We're not witches. God, we worship God not the Devil."

Loud jeers and taunts from the growing crowd of several hundred drowned out his pitiful begging. The cheering grew louder as the brothers were handed up to be tied. Franz was struck dumb and Pawl cried in silence. Some women shouted above the cheering, to limit the small child's pain. One man grabbing him broke his neck, leaving the limp body hanging like a marionette. The flames raced through the mix of dry and oil saturated wood. The intense heat caused the nearest members of the crowd to push back in retreat. But they stayed and watched until the stench of burning flesh brought up the stomach contents of a few.

The charred remains were carried off, for a cost, and dumped into the river. This is what they did with witches long ago, perhaps even today and might do tomorrow. Man, woman or child, younger than a year or very old, if the townsfolk found you to be a witch, you died.

Lust

"Beyond the shadow of a doubt, Brandon is the best person for the job. He's an electronic photography wizard with many photographic awards," Edward Belham assured Polly Prange world-renowned beauty and his newest star. Brandon would locate and catch the peeping tom that sent her naked pictures of herself and demanded money to keep them from being published. "This reprobate shouldn't be paid a cent of ransom to stop pursuing, stalking and embarrassing you."

Brandon acknowledged his boss's compliments. His voice cracked when he asked Miss Prange a few questions about the photos in his shaking hands. He said the pictures were excellent for clarity and focus. The perpetrator knew his business. Had Miss Prange any idea as to where the photos were taken? Her negative answer brought a disappointed frown to Brandon's face. Finally he promised to help, requesting permission for access to her home, studio quarters and the house where she vacationed.

Brandon arrived at the Prange house at noon the following day. Before beginning his search of the house for possible hidden cameras, he talked with Polly; she insisted he call her Polly. They discussed some of her earlier, pre-star days, some of the places she visited, her romantic escapades. Soon a relaxed relationship developed between them. He then went back to the original photos. They looked for some clue; a color, a shape or an object in the photos to pinpoint a camera's location.

Brandon started in the master bedroom. He checked the shower stall, requesting Polly enter the stall and move about as she did when showering. She obliged. He asked if she disrobed in the bedroom when preparing for sleep. She showed him how she went about this nightly task. Did she dress and/or shower in the pool cabanas? She showed him again. Was there any other place in the house Polly disrobed? None. Brandon was ready to check out these places for hidden cameras.

Soon he'd locate and remove every camera and install his own fiber optic digital camera. He would add to his private collection of nude photos of Polly Prange.

Cause for Murder

"I screamed, 'Go to hell!' and shot him."

"And why did you scream, 'Go to hell!' at your husband and shoot him?"

"He hit me and was going to hit me again," she said quietly. There were no tears in the red, swollen eyes, or sorrow as they looked into the limpid blue eyes of her lawyer. The gaunt unsmiling face stared forward, the thin folded hands pressing down into her lap didn't twitch and her voice, soft as it spoke, held no malice.

The judge, sitting next to the woman on the stand, barely heard her words and knowing the jury could not have heard them said, "Mr. Tanner, would you ask your client to speak a little louder, please."

"Yes, your Honor."

"Evelyn. Mrs. Cooper, would you repeat what you just said, only louder and say it to the jury."

Evelyn Cooper, admitted murderer of Burt Cooper, said, "He hit me and was going to hit me again."

There were people in the courtroom other than the jury that hadn't heard the first answer and they reacted to the answer with murmuring. The judge tapped his gavel twice and the murmuring ceased. Not a face in the jury seemed to react to the answer. The newspeople scribbling their notes left no doubt they heard the answer. Attorney William Tanner had known the answer before he asked the question and seemed satisfied with the various reactions in the courtroom, except for the jurors. No reaction from them.

That happened this morning, now he rested at home. The verdict of not guilty, freed his client. For the moment he relaxed and thought back to seven months ago. Mrs. Burt Cooper, Evelyn, called his office and requested he be her attorney. After their initial meeting, hearing the facts not published in the newspapers or bantered about by the television newspeople, he accepted his new client and began digging into the sordid story of the Coopers.

Marion Spokes, his secretary of four years, typed Evelyn's uninterrupted story into a folder on her computer. Then, after Mr. Tanner's interview, she ran off a copy of Mr. Tanner's questions and Evelyn's answers. She also prepared documents, as they began to accumulate, from data found by the paralegals Mr. Tanner employed to research cases that might have a bearing on this case. William Tanner went over all of this detail by detail, summoning every aspect of his legal skills in preparing the best defense possible for Mrs. Cooper. He requested one delay before going to trial.

Evelyn Carpenter married Burt Cooper five months after they met at a Christmas party held at a friend of a friend's house. She was an assistant manager of a small shoe franchise in the newest mall off the tollway, he was a systems analyst for a Midwest trucking firm. Both were into raising tropical fish, enjoyed local theatrical performances, worked out at a health club and neither had a close relationship with their families.

According to Evelyn's statement, about three weeks after their marriage she was talking to a utility man in the hallway of their condo. Getting off the elevator, Burt saw them talking and stalked toward them. Shoving Evelyn into their place he demanded to know why she was talking to him and about what. Completely befuddled by his behavior, she didn't answer quickly enough; he accused her of lying and slapped her across the face.

Stunned, Evelyn ran into the bathroom and locked the door. Burt, hurrying after her, pounded on the door and pleaded for her to forgive him, claiming a fit of jealousy caused his reaction and he loved her very much. Furthermore he promised never to behave like that again. He took her out to dinner and they had a wonderful night of passionate sex, though Burt bruised her breasts by squeezing them too hard in foreplay.

When Evelyn answered the phone one evening and walked into another room while talking, Burt wanted to know who was calling and why. It was her boss she told him and he wanted her to work late tomorrow night. He took the phone from her and told him to discuss working at work and not bother his wife at home. He also told her boss that she was not available for night work and hung up. When Evelyn protested she might lose her job, Burt accused her of having an affair with her boss and punched her. When she started for the bathroom, Burt blocked her way and smacked her several times, each time harder than the last, and with each blow he insisted she was meeting other men behind his back. She finally locked herself in the bathroom while a cursing Burt, storming out the front door of the condo, yelled a warning that if she left, he'd find her and kill her.

In the early morning Burt returned to knock softly on the door asking if she was all right. When Evelyn said no, he asked if he could make amends by bathing her and could she please forgive him. He said he wasn't really mad at her, but sometimes people take advantage of people and her boss was doing that to her. He knew because, well, like in that play they saw, remember? He couldn't think of the name of it but she must remember it. She stood before the medicine cabinet mirror looking at bruises, scrapes, a small shiner and a cut and swollen lip but, wanting to believe him, she finally unlocked the door. Embracing her, he begged her to forgive him. With her yes, he picked her up and hustled her into bed for a morning quickie. She had no say in this. He told her to stay home and he'd fix things for her at work, besides since she had fallen down and injured her face, she wouldn't want to talk to people anyway. Evelyn agreed she would stay home today.

Burt telephoned at 10:00 am and again at 11:30 am to see how she was feeling. He had talked to her boss about work, all taken care of he said. At 3:15 pm he called to tell her what he wanted for dinner. She told him she did not have the ingredients, but he insisted she do her very best and he would stop for two of the items she had to have. He complained after the meal that it wasn't "just right", that she could do better. Oh, sure he managed to agree that the meal was adequate. Then he dropped this bombshell.

He told her boss she was quitting her job to stay home and be a housewife. A quick warning of a kick in the ass if she started bellyaching about it shut off Evelyn's attempt to protest. What was there to protest, she had no job. Later, when the phone rang, Burt answered it and told the other party Evelyn wasn't there and he didn't know when she would be returning. When she reached out for the phone, he hung up and pulling his fist back made a threatening gesture.

Evelyn asked who it was and was told, "That bitchy friend of yours, the one I really don't like, Loree. I don't want you seeing her any more."

"But she's the only..."

"Stay away from her or I'll or ... or. You know what might happen." Burt got up and went over hugging her, talking softly into her ear, telling her she was all that mattered, that he loved her and wanted her all for himself. Just the same Evelyn managed to talk to Loree on the phone, real quick, 'cause Burt would call lottsa times to ask about things, like what was she doing. If the phone was busy he'd keep calling until she answered, wanting to know who she was talking to. Sometimes he'd leave work and come home. One time he got very angry and hit her, knocked her down, breaking her wrist and some fingers. He gets real mad if she doesn't answer the phone right away, but if he's home sometimes he lets it ring and tells her not to answer it.

William Tanner remembered every item mentioned; every beating, every threat, and every action his client endured over the three years of their marriage. Knowing them he made the jury see them as a danger to the life of his client and won his case. Oh, he needed the hospital and doctor's reports too. Tanner closed the folder and his eyes hoping this sordid slice of life would leave his brain. Right now, sleep was what he wanted, but his wife wanted something else.

After undressing in the bedroom she grabbed his manhood firmly, telling him he'd be very sorry if he didn't please her tonight. Bending over to pull back the bed covers he received several stinging, sharp smacks on his bare buttocks.

Glass Angel

The usually boisterous lunch table whispered solemnly of Marta's death. The second grader had died during the night.

"She's an angel now."

"No, you nut. She'll become a ghost, for now."

"Why a ghost?" asked Erin, Marta's best friend.

"Because, when you first die you don't know where heaven is, so you wait. Until you get to heaven, you're a ghost."

"Who says?"

"My big brother says."

Erin moped alone in her room after school. Thoughts and memories of Marta flew in and out of her bewildered mind.

"Troubled?" asked her mom. "About Marta?"

"What is dying?" asked Erin brushing the back of her hand across her tear filled face.

"Honey it's difficult to explain, to anyone. Dying is the end of life. It's the first step into heaven." She dabbed the tears from Erin's puffy face. "It was time for Marta to go to heaven. Don't think about it for now."

"But she can't go to heaven yet. She will become a ghost first."

"No. No sweetheart. Marta was a good girl. Ghosts are never nice kids."

"But some of the kids at school say so."

"They're wrong. They're too young, as you are, to know about heaven and ghosts."

"But Mom."

"That's over. Subject closed. We'll visit the funeral tonight. Clean up."

The odor of burning candles assailed Erin's nose as she entered the funeral parlor. Dimpled yellow flames punctuated a wall showing beribboned baskets of colorful flowers cascading behind the small reddish metal casket. Church-like music quietly wafted about the groups of people standing, two or three together. Animated speakers were saying nothing that could be heard outside their cluster. Empty rows of fancy folding chairs stood before the casket, theater style. Erin held tight to her parents' hands looking for answers to unasked questions. Hesitant, yet with determination, Erin stepped up to the white pleated opening in the casket and peered in. Marta lay there sleeping. Her folks had said she died. She had gone to heaven. But she lay before her, asleep. It confused Erin. She looked to her folks who stood behind her, their crying eyes shut.

Unsure, Erin whispered, "Marta." Her hand reached in to awaken the sleeper. Marta's hand now felt like a glass of cold milk. Erin jerked at the icy touch, a small gasp was exhaled into the scented air. Marta remained still. Marta's mom hugged Erin, her tears flowing into Erin's hair and down her back.

"I want you to keep coming to our house Erin. To see me and maybe talk about—to remember Marta."

Marta's mother turned back to the casket, falling to her knees, a trembling pile of emptiness.

Erin and her parents left as they had come, in silence. They walked home in silence. Even the desperate questions for understanding Erin spoke in silence to herself,

That night, screams. The screams of a tortured child, loud, piercing ripped the comfortable clouds of sleep from the neighborhood. Mr. Fellers, tripped by tangled bedding, fell to the floor, followed by the night table lamp and alarm clock. Mrs. Fellers flew past him to Erin's room.

Asleep in the old coach house, Mr. Ramirez awoke and lurched to the window. He saw lights wink behind drape covered windows in the Feller's house. Ms. L, the neighborhood news service, equating screams with trouble, dialed 911.

"What's wrong Honey? Why are you hollering? Come on. Stop now. Tell me."

Michael Feller stood in the doorway, a trailing sheet embracing his leg.

"Marta's knocking on my window." Sobbing, Erin sucked in air, choking on her fears.

"Sweetheart, you know that's not possible. Remember, we told you, Marta's dead. She's living with God."

Erin's eyes flooding with new tears darted to the window then back to her mom. "I know. But, but I saw her knocking on my window. Like when she calls me to come out. You know?"

Time and soothing words lessened Erin's fears. Quiet settled through the house.

Bang! Bang! Banging on the front door. Red and blue lights danced across the surfaces of Erin's room.

"This is the police. Open this door. What's going on in there? Open this door."

Erin squealed. Loudly.

"Michael, get the door. Tell them the commotion was only a nightmare."

"A nightmare. OK." The white serpentine sheet clung to his retreating foot as he started toward the shouting police. This was the last week of school and already it was too hot to really learn.

Adults, some with coffee cups in hand, waved to the retreating school bus, the yellow container of their dreams and hopes. The group dispersed slowly.

"Didn't sleep well last night Mrs. Feller?" said Mr. Ramirez, bending for the blue plastic wrapped newspaper in the driveway. "Bad dream?"

"Bad dream? Oh, Mr. Ramirez, those children, so much trash in their heads."

"How's that?"

"You heard about the Smidt girl dying? Marta Smidt. Erin's best friend."

"Heard about a school child dying, Ms. L, told me."

"Ghosts, Mr. Ramirez. They told Erin Marta's ghost would visit her."

"Kids'll do that. Did years ago too," the gray bearded gentleman replied.

"She stayed with us all night. Never slept at all. Ghosts."

Mr. Ramirez puttered in his basement all morning. Grinding gears and childish voices brought him out into the afternoon sun.

"Mrs. Feller, if you approve, I have a special someone I want Erin to take home."

Mrs. Feller's head bobbed an affirmative. Erin's red rimmed eyes watched as Mr. Ramirez revealed his treasure; an exquisite figure with a pale pink gown, light blue wings, golden hair and a crystal head wreathed by a wire halo. A stained glass angel filled his hand.

"My grandmother told me, oh, so long ago, about children who die and angels. I made this angel for your window. When your friend, Marta, comes to your window, she wouldn't knock or bother you, instead she will play and talk to your glass angel. Marta will soon be your angel, not a ghost."

"Really? Really, Mr. Ramirez?"

"Yes, little one. Really."

Equals

Let's face it fellas, woman think they are our equals. We are hard pressed at times to either prove it or acknowledge it. Somehow women get to us either in some subtle way or by giving us a simple smack in the head with a two by four.

Example: We, as men, don't mind a little dirt on our bodies. We don't go and wash at once because we figure we'll get dirty again soon enough. Hell, we might get sweaty too, if getting dirty was hard work or play. Then too our beard is a constant complaint, it scratches. Our missing a day of scraping won't kill them, even though they claim it will.

So, how do they get back at us? On a birthday, an anniversary, or for Christmas we receive a brightly wrapped present. The contents of which they deem perfect for us, a bar of sweet smelling soap, or a can of Right Guard or a new electric razor. If their sense of humor is perverse, we get razor blades and a sweet smelling can of shaving cream.

Yes, we love 'em.

When We Don't Understand

Lester walked into the small store just off Milwaukee Avenue. He didn't wish to shop there, but to check out the goods available and see who owned the place. Behind the counter stood a slight oriental woman dressed in the colorful garb of her native country. She raised her head from some needlework and smiled as Lester walked passed her. Lester didn't smile. Without reason he disliked foreigners, especially oriental ones.

Up and down the aisles he walked, just a lot of handicraft goods, some canned foods with foreign names and dried fish and fruit. The dried stuff stinks Lester said to himself. Christ, there couldn't be much to steal in this dump he thought, which is amazing since Lester didn't think too often. Then he saw the electronics display; Sony, Norelco, Toshiba and some American stuff, along with DVDs and CDs.

Lester glanced up into the convex mirror hung in the corner.

Yep, she could see him. He decided to prepare, at least prepare in his mind, then come back and hit the place. He strolled toward the front and the electronic sensor signaled the door to open. He waved to the little figure staring at him as he left the store. When he walked passed the window he saw her hand still under the counter, likely with a finger on an alarm button.

An hour or so later, Lester again scrutinized everything as he entered the store. He took a shopping cart and headed back to the electronics section. He carefully selected the discs he wanted and set them in the cart. Lester even had the gall to check a small slip of paper so the woman could look in the mirror and see he was actually shopping. Well, sort of, the paper was actually one he found on the display counter, garbage from a packing box. Lester could pretend.

Finished, Lester pushed his cart toward the counter. He looked in the mirror behind the counter and saw the wires for an alarm. As the woman tabulated his purchase Lester removed a pair of wire cutters from his jacket and snipped the cord. He grabbed several discs and bolted for the door. It didn't open. The sensor, ever faithful servant, refused to let him out. He had cut all the electricity off in the store.

"Oops." With her hand to her mouth, the old lady giggled. "So sorry."

A Real Man

Royal Marsh figured young Casper Clay was lying, at least some things he claimed he knew were lies. His father may have talked to Jim "Old Gabe" Bridger, renowned mountain man, about the mountain Indians and picked up an odd fact or two about them. Also, he knew very little about the matter of storing thing in the wagons and much less about repairing them. But Royal was desperate for helping hands in his wagon train of forty-two transporting eighty-one people plus the livestock. Plus the young man did seem willing to learn. At least learn certain things. If he'd pay more attention to the wagons than shooting at targets or game and missing, reducing the train's meals, he'd be of more value.

"Casper, stop wasting your ammunition on targets and start providing some meat for everyone's cooking pot."

"Well now listen Mr. Royal, I told you I wanted to be a good shot, I gotta practice. Who knows how many Indians will attack

this train. I'll be ready to shoot them all. Kill all them dirty animals."
He drew his revolver, "Bang, bang, bang, kill them all. I'll kill an
Indian one day."

"Listen my young friend, you kill nobody. These people are
not our enemies and are not at war with us. They're just different
people, friendly and helpful, leave them in peace."

"Until they want something and they kill us first to get it."

"Stay away from them. If Indians come around you get off
somewhere away from them." Royal was angry and desperate to
accomplish a good trip through the upper Missouri River country, a
safe trip. "You cause trouble with the Indians and so help me I'll
shoot you myself."

"Ain't nice to talk like that."

"And it ain't nice for you to go on with your killing Indian
talk."

Lazarus Booth saw the first signs of Indians about. Like any
scout worth his salt, he determined who, how many and what they
were doing. Then he talked it over with the wagon train captain,
Royal Marsh. The Indians were a group of elderly women and men
no longer connected with their tribe, but left to fend for themselves
until they died. It was a tribal custom, giving the young people a
better chance to survive. Begging was an honest means of surviving.
They also bartered for goods.

Lazarus understood the language of this group and soon had
them setting their camp up away from the settlers and the wagons.
He told the Indians some trading might take place that evening, but
both camps should keep their people out of the others' camp. It
was agreed.

The settlers began searching for buffalo chips to burn for heat
and to cook their food. The Indians did likewise. Casper Clay sat
on the wagon seat watching two Indians moving back and forth in
their search, and one settler doing the same. The three came together
and reached for the same object. The settler reared back. Clay fired

one shot and one Indian fell. The second shot missed and so did the third.

In moments the peace was threatened. Royal Marsh ran out between the two groups. Lazarus joined him and stopped the Indians from advancing on the wagon train.

"What the hell happened?" he asked Lazarus.

"I'm not sure. But there is a wounded Indian on the ground over there," he said pointing toward the small cluster of weeping and chanting Indian women. "I think that damn fool Casper shot an Indian."

Marsh threw his hat to the ground and screamed, "Casper Clay, Get your sorry being over here, right here, right now."

"I'm here," shouldering his rifle across the back of his neck. "I shot the Indian because he was attacking one of our people."

"Who? How? My God, man, who was the Indian attacking?"

"Him. Conroy."

"Conroy, set your rifle down and walk over here."

With a few steps Conroy stood before Royal Marsh. "I didn't see what happened."

"Did the Indian attack you? Threaten you? Are you hurt?"

"No, he didn't attack me. Nor threaten me. Nor am I hurt."

Royal pivoted about driving his fist into Casper's grinning face. The other fist did likewise. The combination punches sent the young man reeling back into a wagon wheel. Casper Clay lay on the ground oblivious to his surroundings. The Indian elders surmised the reason for Royal's behavior. In their present position they had been unable to act with haste and send for warriors to come and destroy the entire wagon train.

When the young Clay awoke some time later, he found himself lashed to a rock, cold and naked. The wagons were gone but the creaking of their wheels carried to his ears a significant message, "We have left you behind." The slow methodical beat of several drums also carried a message from the Indian encampment. "We are here to give you justice."

Where Is the Truth

Once again in the Federal Courts defendant Mother Goose has failed to provide sufficient proof to her claim that all the nursery rhymes and stories published under her name are hers alone. The affidavits sworn to before Judge Knott by many children that Mrs. Goose stole their stories has yet to be submitted as evidence. The trial is now set for February 14th allowing both parties more time for heart to heart negotiations.

Judge Knott instructed lawyers in this class action suit against author Mother Goose to bring in positive proof of plagiarism. Claims by their clients using marginal notes and quotes do not indicate complete stories. Clarification of ownership by more explicit documentation is needed. On the way to his chambers the court clerk told the judge that someone claimed Moses didn't have the title to the tablets.

Waiting Room

I sit. I wait. I listen for any sound, or watch the clerk in the pink coat at the service desk checking people as they come in and the others already waiting. Somehow I notice the air is different, pleasantly cool, and the free, fresh brewed coffee tastes different. Checking my watch, I see I've been waiting ten minutes. It seems longer.

Coming here Bea, my wife, and I didn't discuss her impending surgery. Too early, quarter of six, or were we lost in worries? The doctor's reassurances left doubts here and there. I admit I looked for them. I prayed, it's a universal source of comfort.

The girl in pink called a name. It sounded like mine. Two of us walk to the tiny desk. "Mr. Flynn?" queries the confused woman.

"Sorry. I thought I heard Quinn. I'm Quinn," smiling, I turn back to my seat now occupied by someone thumbing through an ancient magazine. I settle into another chair.

A petite pregnant child stands in the doorway. Lost? Confused? She plods to the reception desk, whispers, and is directed to a row of chairs. She'll be uncomfortable there. Others, who watched her progress, now return to their magazines, reveries or sleep.

The wall clock is slow, working, I can hear the ticking, but slow. Eighteen minutes since Bea left with the green suited nurse. Funny, as they went through the swinging doors the white corridor and walls beyond were a different world.

More names are called, conferences between waiting people and doctors are muted and dance-like. There are smiles and tears. Unintentionally, a voice rises to question the doctor's statements, then fades. They become mannequins on a silent stage.

The eternal questions being asked and answered, "When do they die?" The consoled and inconsolable. One hour. It seemed like four. The swinging doors allow a woman to pass through. Behind her, in the alien white world, I see the doctor. Coming into the room he beckons, walking toward me. I don't like the set of his jaw, or his smile. Feeble?

"Mr. Quinn you may or may not know that the hospital had an emergency. A bad accident. Many of the doctors worked on it. Your wife is sedated and comfortable. I'm going in to her now. You must wait a while longer. Sorry. Any questions? Oh, I told the nurse I would tell you about this delay, as you may not have known what was happening."

"No questions. Perhaps I could get a bite to eat. Okay?"

"Sure. You know where the cafeteria is, go there. I'll send word to you there if you wish."

Sitting here is different. Dishes clinking, the soft murmur of voices, the louder bantering of the kitchen workers, even the sunlight trying to peek through the wire- embedded glass is pleasant. Radiant heat. Warm. Soothing.

A disembodied hand and head poke through the door opening, "Mr. Quinn? Is there a Mr. Quinn here?"

I raised my coffee. Dripping drops became little sunbursts on the table.

"Follow me please."

I quickened my pace to be at her side. "She done? Everything okay?"

"I don't know sir. I'm just a gopher." Smiling, she said, "Your doctor will meet with you in here." She slipped a folder into the basket on the door she held open for me. She was gone.

More waiting. A small room with a copy of Dunne's painting called The Guardian Angel. No books, magazines or pamphlets and worse, no windows. With bars, painted or real, it was a damn nice cell.

The door opened. The folder in the doctor's hands also opened, like magic.

"Good news on a leash."

"Huh?"

"Everything in surgery went as planned. We sent a small polyp to the lab for a biopsy. The lab isn't sure of the test and is redoing it. It's like getting a second opinion."

"Does that happen often?"

"Often enough. We need fifteen, twenty minutes more here," the doctor said. "We wait."

"But she is okay? Nothing is wrong?"

"I think so. Usually these tests are negative. That's good news."

"Okay."

He handed me a pill. "This has been a long day. You were up early and I want you to relax. This will help if you wish to take it."

I closed my hand around the tablet, "Thank you."

"I'll be back in a bit."

As the door closed, I was alone again with my worries and sensing a worse day coming.

Forecast

Concentrating on the local weather, Cool Waters, the weatherman in the Santa suit, gave tonight's weather summation. However his mind was on his planned burglary of a neighbor.

"A nip in the air should have late shoppers shivering a bit. Today's humidity is already dissipating. It'll be a moonless night without wind. Tomorrow's high forty-seven." Cool smiled and waved giving a rolling "Ho, ho, ho."

Jimmy Lane, the neighbor living kitty-corner to Cool's backyard home in Antioch, was an electronic games nut. Jimmy invited Cool and a few other neighborhood men into his computer/game room two weeks ago, where Cool fell in love with everything he saw. He had to have some of these games. He'd buy them but the recent divorce had cleaned out his bank account.

The next day he nearly got arrested for attempting to boost an iPod from an electronics store. Remaining calm, he convinced the store manager, who recognized the local weatherman, that he intended to pay for it and only placed it in his jacket pocket so he could examine a headset. He was walking out of the store without paying because he forgot the iPod in his pocket. He decided then to pay Jimmy a visit and casually appropriate some of his things.

Cool remembered hearing Jimmy mention that on Christmas Eve he would be at his brother's place in Mundelein. The family usually went to midnight mass, had a small bite to eat then opened presents. If things went as usual the Lanes would get home around three in the morning. Cool would have what he wanted by then.

Breathing in deep, filling his lungs with the crisp night air, Cool exhaled a cloud of vapor which froze into diamond crystals before his face then silently dropped to the ground. Crunching his way directly to Jimmy's house, Cool Waters punched in the patio door. The Christmas tree lights lit the computer room and the things Cool wanted flew into his hands. Rushing the loot back to his place, he made a second trip, taking a new computer with a large red bow from under Jimmy's giant TV.

"What the hell?" Cool cursed aloud as the doorbell's jangling called him from his sleep. "Just a damn minute. I'm coming. I'm coming," he shouted out at the ringing bell and bounced in an awkward rolling motion down the steps. Pulling open the ice frosted door, "Whattaya bas..." Silence came from his open mouth as he looked into the faces of two large policemen.

"Mr. Waters?"

"Yes."

"It's quite chilly Mr. Waters. May we... Hey you're the weatherman," the policeman paused in mid-sentence.

"Uh huh. I'm your weatherman. And I predicted cold."

"Mr. Waters, can we step in to speak to you? It'll be warmer."

"Yeah. Sure. Come in, come in."

"Mr. Waters," said the officer who seemed to be in charge. "There was a burglary at the Lane house sometime last night."

"My God. No one hurt I hope."

"Nope, Just a burglary," the other policeman said. "We're collecting statements, some information that might help solve the burglary. Did you hear or see anything last night sir?"

"No. Nothing. I'm a pretty heavy sleeper. Don't even get up for nature during the night."

"Can you see the Lane house from this house?" asked the policeman in charge.

"From the back you can."

"May we see, sir?"

The two policeman followed Cool into the next room. Cool pulled the drapes open and looked toward Lane's across the yard. He fell to his knees blubbering, "Oh no. No, no, no."

Across the yards from Lane's place to his house and back again were two distinct sets of footprints captured in the crystalline white frost carpeting the entire area. Jimmy Lane stood at the patio door shaking his fist and hollering. "Merry Christmas, Cool. You forgot to predict frost."

A Different Telling of A Familiar Story

"I think we underestimated the number of people that would show up."

"I didn't expect such a mob Matthew," John said. "I don't think any of us did."

"Got any ideas?"

"About what?" came John's perplexed response.

"Well. Like feeding them."

John, turning in a complete circle, threw up his hands. "Why feed them? They can take care of themselves, like they always do."

"Not this time, Buddy. I believe Someone asked them to gather here."

"No. He didn't?"

"Why don't you go ask Him what we should do?"

Returning, with a puzzled smile twisting his face, John went directly to Matthew. "Peter said not to worry. Some guy on the other side of the group had some fish and bread. He donated them and they're passing the stuff out now."

"Gee. I hope there's enough. I'm hungry."

Reprisal

Margo Hauptmann heard the heavy trucks coming down the road before she saw them. Smiling inwardly and stepping onto the small stoop, she stared indifferently as the three vehicles turned onto the main street and stopped. She recognized the Commandant and knew what would happen and what he had to say. She could hear him from where she stood.

Speaking to herself, *"The trucks'll seal off the street. The soldiers will quickly herd the citizens off the sidewalks onto the street toward the Commandant's car. There they go. Don't they ever change? Now he'll try to intimidate them."*

Margo heard him begin his accusation and moved off the stoop. It was about time to intimidate him she thought. She moved through the the immobile, shocked group. They gasped at the Commandant's order. She could feel their desire to run and the panic sweeping through the crowd when they realized they were trapped.

Moving out from the shrinking throng, Margo dared to speak. The silent, desperate people were bewildered by her audacity. They were horrified when the Commandant struck her and ordered her shot too.

Margo knew what she wanted done at that moment. She knew exactly what she wanted done. At her signal, a raised fist, the windows in the upper floors of the surrounding buildings flew open. The fist came down and the soldiers were shot dead in their ranks. Margo had sprung her trap.

She hastened to the fallen Commandant, reached down and retrieved the weapon from his holster. Calmly she shot him in the head and then sent the gathered throng home with orders to lock themselves in and forget the incident. As if they could.

Her compatriots gathered the weapons then stripped the bodies. The dead were carried off and thrown into an abandoned mine, the car driven into a nearby mountain lake. When they had failed to steal arms from a supply area last night, Margo left incriminating clues and a dead soldier. The enemy rushed to retaliate only to fall into her trap.

Caladrius

Russell Peers spent several minutes looking at the painting in the book. His father, pointing to the oddly shaped bird said, "That bird on the beds is a Caladrius, Rusty." He never called him Russell. "A long time ago people believed if you were sick and this bird looked at you it would cure you."

"Looks weird."

"Maybe to you. It played an important part in the life of the King of Jerusalem, Baldwin the IV. I want you to understand that it might become important in your life too."

"How?"

A few days ago Rusty sat with his parents listening to the oncologist tell them his lungs were infected with cancer cells. Nine years old, Rusty didn't quite understand what that meant, but both of his parents were dabbing at their eyes to control the flow of tears.

Now John Peers, an admirer of the crusades and crusaders, was going to read a story to his son. He had prepared Rusty to hear some stories before they arrived at the Art Institute Library. But right now he felt a certain trembling in his knees. He had discussed the matter with Helen, his wife of eleven years, and they agreed to present the boy with a story that would give him some hope. John Peers chose the story of the fabled Caladrius, saviour of the sick. Sitting in a small corner, Rusty listened as his father began reading.

"Father! Father! Look, I'm getting the best of him." The young prince and his instructor were clashing their wooden swords in an indoor arena. Circling about each other, they were attempting to strike a telling blow. "I'll have him."

"Good. Good. Watch what you are..." the king said, then gasped as the opponent's stick came down on the right shoulder of his son. "He outmaneuvered you."

The boy hadn't flinched at a blow so hard that the padding slid down his arm. "Never even felt it."

Both the king and the teacher stood looking at the swelling, reddened welt and the trickle of blood on the upper muscle. The lesson stopped when the king prompted, "Best have the surgeon take a look. You know your mother will have a fit if she thinks you're hurt. You say you didn't feel the blow?"

"Nope. I don't feel pain, never in my right arm."

"Odd," the king clasped the boy's shoulder and squeezed. "No pain?"

"No pain."

Afterward, the king's surgeon sent the boy off to his mother and taking the king aside expressed his opinion. "I gave the lad a few pinches which he could not see. It is my opinion my lord the prince has leprosy."

The shock of hearing this horrible news popped the royal mouth open nearly as wide as his eyes. The quaver in his voice indicated how significant this pronouncement was. Leprosy would mean isolation for the prince, even an early death. Worse, he would never be king. "How can we be sure?"

"You will not want anyone to know of this sire. I will discreetly inquire of an associate or two and get their opinions."

"Yes, do that. Is there no other way to be sure?"

"You must, by often touching him in the area when he isn't looking, find out if he feels pain. Leprosy deadens the part or parts of the body stricken by the disease."

"How am I to know if I must touch him without his knowing?"

"Your Majesty, could you not pretend to talk to the boy with your hands on both shoulders, gradually pressing more firmly and as you do and watch his face for grimaces?"

Pausing before he answered, the king agreed with a nod of his head.

In time the surgeon's suspicions were confirmed, the young prince had leprosy. His parents were devastated. Close advisors urged the king to select a kinsman to assume the crown should it be necessary, it was only a suggestion with weight. The king died before designating anyone and Baldwin IV mounted the throne at thirteen, with two regents, one was his uncle, to assist him in governing Jerusalem.

It wasn't long before the boy was told of his problem and the possible consequences that things changed from the somber attitude of the ruling family to that of a happier family. The disease did weaken the prince at times and he would retire for a nap. One mid-afternoon his screaming alerted the household and those within the sound of the screams ran to his room. It took a moment, but his uncle, seeing nothing but a smiling boy lying in bed, sent the unneeded assembly about their duties. His sister, mother, uncle and the royal surgeon gathered about the bed and listened to the tale the boy told.

"I assure you I am not retelling you a dream. But I wish to have a priest come before I tell you what happened."

"Sibylla, go to the chapel. Get Father Abrim. Ask him to bring the host and wine when he comes. Hurry girl," said her mother. "Baldwin lie back and rest, you look so different."

"Must we wait son? Surely you may tell us something," the regent said.

Baldwin, smiling, put his finger to his lips, "We must wait."

Out of breath, the priest followed Sibylla into Baldwin's bedchamber. Kneeling next to the bed, he placed the wine and bread on the small table and turned to the boy. "Do you need the Last Rites? Is this why you have called for me?"

A glow lit his face and his mouth parted with a smile, his hand reaching out to touch the priest's. "No, my friend. No. No. I think I have experienced a miracle."

In the silence of the room several gasps were audible. Several heads turned to seek out if others heard the same word, "Miracle." The priest crossed himself and mumbled, "Agnus Dei."

"Hmmm," droned his uncle. "A miracle. What makes you think you experienced a miracle?"

"Father will tell us if a miracle has happened when he hears my story. Straightening himself into an upright position on the bed, Baldwin coughed then began. "I had fallen asleep and when I attempted to shift about, I felt a heavy weight upon my chest. It was difficult to breath and I reached out to brush the weight away. My hand struck a solid object which moved ever so little that it still weighed upon my chest. Opening my eyes I saw a bird as big as a laying hen looking at me. It was pure white, whiter than the doves that roost in the temple walls. It cocked its head looking into my face then hopped up and flew out that window." Baldwin pointed to a shuttered aperture. "But it was closed."

The priest crossed himself again, muttering more Latin invocations. Still kneeling he questioned the boy. "As big as a laying hen?"

"About."

"Pure white? Every feather?"

"I saw none but white ones," licking his lips. "Yes, all white."

"You did not leave your bed to close the shutter?"

"The boy would not lie Father," interjected the regent.

"Please, it is not a lie I seek."

His mother, having kneeled when the priest entered the room, asked from her position at the foot of the bed, "Is it a miracle, Father?"

"Perhaps. I will write to the Bishop to find out if it is a miracle." Standing, he continued, "I have often heard that the sick may be visited by a pure white bird, the Caladrius. It is said that if the bird looks at you it will draw out your illness and fly off carrying it to the sun where it is dropped and burns into ash. It means the sick person will become well."

"I have heard of the Caladrius," the queen replied as she rose to her feet. "Might our son be cured? How will we know?"

"Woman stop asking questions until the priest can give us answers."

"We will know soon enough. We need only to pinch the infected area. If there is pain, he has been cleansed and freed of his leprosy."

Contrary to the desires of the seers, friends, doctors and family, leprosy did not leave his body. However, he became King Baldwin the IV and reigned for eleven years.

They called him their king. He behaved as a benevolent king. He led them in battle against the people down river that had attempted to steal their reserves of food. He accepted gifts from the visitors wishing to pass through his lands and distributed these gifts among his people. Yes he could be called king, for lack of a better title.

Rusty didn't understand the reason for the story, but then what nine-year-old would?

It Really Happened

July 7th and Washington, D.C. was hot. Mary didn't belong with these three men; Herold, Powell or Atzerodt. Nearly every man in the crowd thought she shouldn't be there. Something would change her situation any moment now she thought.

She didn't want to see what was happening. Thoughtfully, someone had covered her eyes. She didn't like being trussed up hand and foot either. She did appreciate her dress being wrapped around her ankles. Modesty was a factor and she didn't want people staring and pointing if her dress came above her ankles, even accidentally. Mary heard a muffled command and felt the floor beneath fall away.

The four conspirators swung and twisted at the end of the gallows ropes. They had murdered Abraham Lincoln and died for it. Mary Surratt became the first woman to be tried by the Federal government and executed in America.

Suddenly

Easing out of the restrictive confines of my winter covering, I continued pumping my new energy into the brightest, most colorful appendages I'd ever seen. Swatches of black and yellow waving at my command extended out from my back. I felt their power pulling me up and off the faded wrapping that held me hidden from my enemies through the winter. I was flying, leaving the only home I ever knew, from egg to butterfly. Now I'm free.

Let's see, send out my scent, mate and lay my eggs on a— Hey! What? What's happening? Why have I stopped just a flap or two into the air? Something has grabbed me. Ouch! There's a sharp pain as a metal pin punctures my body and fastens me to a board. Seeing through these eyes is tricky, but I see a label on the pin; Papilio podalirius. Mmmmm. I think I've become a collector's item.

Don't Mess With Tradition

Conner and Esther Burns didn't indicate or bother to tell the tour company or their companion tourists they were eloping newlyweds and this trip was their honeymoon. Their behavior betrayed them however, but their fellow travelers allowed them their deception. Both of them were enthusiastic about the arranged trips and exotic sights. They took part in the cruise ship activities and danced and played in the casino until the wee hours. Today their group would tour an ancient temple site steeped in mythological stories of bloody sacrifice and lustful orgies.

"My god, the climb is enough to kill you," Conner gasped as he and Esther reached the top of the ancient Indian pyramid. He flopped onto the stone step, sucking mightily for air.

Giggling and exuberant, his bride collapsed next to him. "I hope I can make you this exhausted tonight," and kissing him hard showed what she intended. "Come on, let's go down and see some more." She tugged at his shoulder. "Come on."

"Wait a moment. Did you believe that guy when he said the spirits of the sacrificed maidens haunt this place?"

Shrugging her shoulders Esther said, "Well I'd damn well like to come back and avenge myself if I were a sacrifice."

"Really? You believe that kind of nonsense?"

"I didn't say that. I said I'd like to avenge myself." Esther emphasized her point with a cat-like striking motion. "Those virgin girls still had a lot to live for and some men slaughtered them, I'm sure against their will, when they were just looking forward to life. Shame, shame." She stood and stretching toward her husband, gave a little tug.

As Conner got to his feet, Esther began her long, screaming fall into eternity. Over and over, her body bounced from one stone step to another until a nearly bloodless, but severely bruised young body crumpled into a bloody pile on the ancient stone floor of the plaza at the bottom of the pyramid. Conner didn't try to move. Watching his bride tumbling down caused him to scream but not to move. When his locked muscles did function and he started down the steps he nearly fell too.

Now, three months after the inquest which determined Esther's death was an accident, Conner entered the law offices of Rios and Gonzales to claim his inheritance. Absolutely no one knew that Conner had chased Esther Hess for the Hess fortune. The gold sales and refining process Abner Hess built into a seventy million dollar business he passed along to his only daughter two years ago. While atop the pyramid Conner Burns had given her a slight shove as she attempted to assist him to his feet. It suited his get rich quick plans when this opportunity occurred.

Juan Rios, Mexico's popular soccer star of a decade ago and now a flourishing legal star, rose to greet Conner. "Welcome to Mexico."

"Thank you, I didn't know I had to return here. You know— for this will stuff, this reading."

"Yes, strange. "I didn't know either until I read this note." He handed Conner a note smelling slightly of jasmine, Esther's favorite scent. "I found it in the papers when I went to court to file your claim."

Scanning the note Conner said, "So, is there anything preventing me from claiming whatever Esther left me?" he handed the note back.

"One condition. Rather odd, but the courts will tell you must comply to inherit." Senor Rios continued reading silently before returning the letter to Conner.

"It says in her letter you should go back and put flowers at her death site."

"That's it?"

"That's it." Rios leaning back into his plush chair said, "When you called to confirm your appointment, I went out to buy flowers and a one-shot camera. Go out there, leave the flowers and have some tourist take your picture with the newspaper from today. Bring the picture to me and I'll see that the papers are filed and your money will be in your hands in two to three weeks.

The inconvenience bothered Conner, but he took the flowers and camera. Outside he bribed a tour bus driver to take him to the pyramid. He asked a tourist to photograph him with flowers at the bottom of the stone blocks, and then he went to the tiny rest area for a cool drink and waited for the return ride. The heat and humidity overcame him and he dozed in a chaise lounge beneath the souvenir display. Esther was searching for him in his fitful dream, chasing him and driving a poison dart into his heart. This was her revenge and she stood over him watching him slowly choke as the poison shut down his breathing.

The local police didn't understand how a small souvenir doll of a high priest falling from a rack just above the tourist could kill him, but he was dead. The figure fell a few inches and the staple holding the price tag had scratched him. The police report was certain neither object could kill a man; his death was an odd accident. But when the newspeople found out who Conner was and why he was at the pyramid, rumors of the return of an avenging sacrificed maiden became the big news of the day.

Do And Die

Walking, just walking made Andy feel great. After eight months he was looking forward to returning to some of the activities he loved before the bear attack. Andy's bare handed fight to save a child had made him a media hero. The limp, the empty eye socket, the difficulty with digestion and some things the doctors weren't sure of and didn't stress, Andy didn't question. He was leaving the hospital. That was very important. The wheelchair rolled to a stop and Andy stepped toward the waiting car.

The group heard her screams and watched as the purse snatcher barreled by Andy's wheelchair. Instantly and automatically Andy was in pursuit. Running the hurdles got him through college. Muscles honed to perfection before the attack were struggling to respond to Andy's demands. At first they protested but soon complied, albeit, awkwardly. Quickly he was gaining on the thief, gaining, reaching out, out, out. Suddenly darkness.

One of the on duty ER doctors, standing outside the hospital enjoying the spring air, saw what was happening. He hustled to Andy's prone figure and listened for a heart beat. He stood, shaking his head. Still plugged in, the dangling stethoscope shook too. "He's dead."

The newspaper headline read, **Hero Dies in Heroic Effort**. The story on page three says the purse snatcher escaped.

The Powerful Strike Their Enemies

Hands pressing tightly over his ears, de Laubardemont prime persecutor of Urbain Grandier shouted to his aide, "Shut the window, his screams are deafening me and the stench of his burning flesh fouls the air in the room." It had taken one man one year to collect enough evidence from many men to execute an innocent man.

In August 1633, Cardinal Richelieu, sent M. de Laubardemont, his Councilor of State, to Loudun, France. The castle in Loudun was to be destroyed as were many fortified castles Richelieu considered not needed against an invasion. It was part of his plan to suppress feudal nobility and the Huguenot's power while increasing the royal power in France. Things changed in Loudun soon after his arrival.

These things of change actually began a few years earlier. Urbain Grandier was an extremely fortunate young man; in college at age twelve, handsome, multilingual and a priest. His abilities far surpassed the simple folks with whom he had dealt. He was handsome and many men had a tendency to envy him. Because a priest, Père Meunier, lied about him, he sued him and won, making an enemy. Winning a suit against an ambitious, vindictive, hypocritical attorney created more ill feelings.

Père Mignon represented a convent of Ursuline nuns that recently acquired a haunted house in Loudun. Being nuns they bought it cheap figuring spirits wouldn't haunt the religious. However, things got stickier when an uncle of Mignon had words with Urbain about the house payments and words were exchanged making the rich uncle's family worry about their inheritance. Also, it was reported Urbain made a young girl pregnant. She was a niece of Uncle Mignon and her father was a king's attorney. In a small town they had something to talk about. But there's more. Isn't there always?

Urbain's list of enemies grew longer when friends chose sides and repeated stories, often embellishing them. One such self-made man of importance, Duthibaut, was told by Urbain on the steps of the church, in public, to stop his slanderous stories. Duthibaut struck Urbain with his cane. Urbain complained to the king. He sent the priest to the high court of Parliament in Paris for adjudication. While he was in Paris his enemies decided to get him. The King's attorney and several of his ilk went to the advisors of the Bishop at Poitiers with charges against Urbain. These were such things as blasphemy, debauchery and prostitution. The Bishop didn't like Urbain. After reading their report he ordered him arrested for trial.

Well they lied and lied. All their evidence was based on hearsay, yet Grandier was found guilty. Both sides were dissatisfied with the sentence: "Three months of fast each Friday on bread and water by way of penance; to be prohibited from the performance of clerical functions in the diocese of Poitiers for five years, and in the town of Loudun forever." Grandier appealed to the Archbishop of Bordeaux while Duthibaut and company went to the Parliament in

Paris. The whole mess was placed in the hands of a public prosecutor in Poitiers. He was able to find witnesses to admit to taking bribes, and some declared their statements had been changed. Duthibaut was reprimanded and forced to apologize publicly and pay a fine. He gathered his co-conspirators at Trinquant's house to discuss their position, whereupon Mignon made a suggestion all agreed to.

Remember the haunted house the Ursuline nuns bought? Mignon was selected director by them after their director died and their first choice of Urbain Grandier declined the job. The nuns in the beginning of 1626 came mainly from fine families. The founding superior was related to de Laubardemont, one nun was related to Richelieu, and a couple belonged to the family of the Archbishop of Bordeaux.

During their first year there were no haunting reports. Before Mignon stepped in, some of the younger nuns and paying boarders, resenting some of the old regime's rules, started ghostly shenanigans. They were making noises with chains, moaning, crying and even pulling the bedding off sleepers. Soon these pranks were told to Mignon by Mother Superior. He saw an opportunity to exhort these night visitors and make a name for himself. He would have the convent pray, fast and make confessions before exorcising them.

Bingo! Confession. The boarders told of the haunting tricks they were playing. He told Mother Superior explaining that the hauntings should continue since immediate house cleaning would cast doubt of ghosts being there. Gradually reports of ghosts were being told by townsfolk and that Mignon was driving them out. He allowed the rumors to continue. Then he asked a friend, Pe're Barre, to come and see what was happening in the convent. Barre arrived leading many members of his parish and after several hours in the convent sent them home because he was needed here. Within two weeks, the two friends requested, no begged, a priest, a bailiff and a civil lieutenant to come and examine two nuns possessed by demons. By means of exorcism they had found several devils possessing the superior.

The three men were brought into the superior's room already filled with sisters, monks, a priest and a surgeon. They watched the nun convulsing while making grimaces and sounds. Mignon, to prove further evidence of satanic possession informed them his questions would be answered in Latin, a language she didn't know. The questions were worded to blame Grandier. Three of the requested guests weren't overly impressed and Mignon reminded them that what they had just seen was similar to a case that resulted in the execution of a priest. They recognized this attempt to blame Urbain. But seeking more proof, asked Mignon to take them to the other possessed nun and ask the same questions. She couldn't answer.

Now Barre added to the stories by promising to get the devil's name, but not now because the possessed and the demons were tired. Later this afternoon he told them. Then they were told tomorrow morning. Arriving in the morning they were requested to wait and spent an hour waiting in a house removed from the convent. They returned demanding to enter. Barre and Mignon informed them that through their conjuring the nuns were no longer possessed. The men were outraged declaring them under suspicion of collusion, fraud, illegal proceedings and insolence. They answered that they had done the holy work of the church. They wrote up their report but the lieutenant refused to sign it because he believed in the exorcism. He thought, at this point, doubters were proliferating. Things quieted down.

Six weeks later, the evil spirits attacked many occupants of the convent. One of the king's attorneys, even though he was anti-Grandier, ordered the bailiff to tell Barre and Mignon to stop exorcisms unless witnessed by an official or a doctor accompanying the bailiff. They refused his orders stating the prior orders given by the Bishop of Portiers were still in force. They said a letter was coming with further orders but he could see the nuns if they wanted to see him. They refused. The next day the bailiff, with four physicians, went to the convent and were placed in a barred off section of the chapel while the nuns heard mass.

During communion Mother Superior went into convulsions. Barre began speaking in Latin, and she began answering in Latin so filled with grammatical mistakes, it shocked the doctors, and they laughed. When Barre realized the predicament he asked much simpler questions. One doctor, sensing fraud, requested she answer in Greek, for all devils know all languages. Mother Superior returned to her normal self. The little group was taken to the other possessed nun, she began laughing, calling out "Grandier! Grandier!" She spoke in French and used vulgar gestures and words. Barre reverted to Latin and sister's Latin answers were poorer than her superior's. The next day at mass Mother Superior and another nun yelled slanderous remarks against Grandier. When questioned later she came back to her senses, a pattern frequently resorted to when wanting to end the questioning.

Many attempts to secure proof were tried by both sides. The bailiff tried to control and report everything he could. He called together the town's select, asking for help in the public's best interest. The written reports were sent to the Bishop of Poitiers and the attorney general. The latter said it was a church matter and the bishop didn't reply. Barre decided to request a new commission from the bishop. The bishop sent two new commissioners, both related to someone in the group fighting with Grandier. Again, Grandier begged the Archbishop of Bordeaux for help and he, ascertaining the dire straights Grandier was in, sent emissaries at once. They were to conduct exorcisms to end this case once and for all. It did no good, for Barre and Mignon met them at the convent gate telling them they had finally driven the devils out of the convent, the nuns were cured. Albeit the notoriety had parents withdrawing their boarding offspring thereby reducing their income and new novices.

In 1633, Richelieu, having already demolished many castles, set about the destruction of Loudun castle. His appointed agent, M. deLaubardemont, arrived in town to meet with the town prefect, Memin de Silly, an old friend of the Cardinal and an admirer of Barre and Mignon. The newly arrived big shot was partied and introduced to Mignon and his friend. Mother Superior, a relative of de Laubardemont, was also there. One of the incidents talked about concerned Richelieu. It referred to a time when he held little power and the Queen mother detested him. The teller of the story was a friend of Grandier.

The time was ripe. Would de Laubardemont visit the convent? Surely the devils would return and impress the dignitaries by possessing some nuns, and this would show their power over God. The nuns were attacked with violent convulsions which de Laubardemont alluded to when he returned to Paris. Richelieu remembered Grandier had once bested him in an argument over etiquette. He disliked that and wanted revenge. To wit, he gave orders for Grandier's arrest and all officers of the king would assist in the arrest and trial. Even those few that sided with Grandier, seeing it was a royal order, removed themselves from a position that could be interpreted as pro Grandier.

The case was building, and more nuns became possessed. The sister of Memin was to keep the nuns apart. The attending doctors were the least skilled in town. The apothecary was Mignon's cousin, already convicted of prescribing the wrong drugs and killing a patient. The surgeon was Mannouri, nephew of de Silly and brother of a nun. The Bishop of Poitiers discharged Richelieu's exorcists and appointed his own chaplain, Père Lactance, who had passed the sentence of the first trial. He saw Mother Superior had no knowledge of Latin so ordered the demon to speak in French. To hasten the proceedings, the doctors went to various other locations, saw convulsions and odd behavior and concluded demons were in possession of these nuns.

At one point the Superior said Grandier entered her as various animals and that he had five devil marks on him. Mannouri was ordered to shave Grandier's body, finding a spot on the shoulder and one on the thigh. He began using a probe with a hollow handle allowing a needle to enter the body or slide back when Mannouri applied it to the spots or other body parts. Blindfolded, Grandier was surprised by the stab of the needle the first time and he screamed. Repeated stabbings produced no more screams. M. de Laubardemont watched it all.

It is a known fact to the people living in 1633 that devils know all languages and where a person is at all times. The possessed nuns couldn't speak the languages their observers requested nor locate Grandier. Tests were promised for the next evening. Several people questioned why at night instead of the usual morning hour. To prove demons possessed the convent, Mother Superior would rise off her bed, de Laubardemont's hat would leave his head and hang in the air, and six strong men would not be able to hold down a petite possessed nun. When the nun appeared to float up from her bed, a man peeking under her dress saw her to be on her tip toes. A couple of fellows saw de Laubardemont sit under the bell tower and found a man holding a line with a hook sitting above de Laubardemont, his hat remained on his head. A single man challenged the six strong men and held the nun down by himself. Père Lactance and de Laubardemont were beside themselves as they saw their attempts fail.

Père Lactance predicted that on the 20th of May, three demons would leave Mother Superior's body and no one would see them. Doctors examined her before the exorcism started. The exorcism would be performed for the many people that had traveled from afar to see the miracle. Mother Superior was questioned and answered in French. She went into convulsions and fell to the floor. When she was lifted, her clothing was cut in three places and three wounds were found. But wait, tiny scratches were found on her body and her finger tips were bloody. The doctors felt she hid tiny blades under her fingernails but de Laubardemont wouldn't allow an opinion into the report.

Many, many people differed with what they witnessed, too many in the judgment of the Archbishop. So the following notice was issued. "All persons, of whatever rank or profession, are hereby expressly forbidden to traduce, or in any way malign, the nuns and other persons at Loudun possessed by evil spirits; or their exorcists, or those who accompany them either to the places appointed for exorcism or elsewhere; in any form or manner whatever, on pain of a fine of ten thousand livres, or a larger sum and corporal punishment should the case so require; and in order that no one may plead ignorance hereof, this proclamation will be read and published to-day from the pulpits of all the churches, and copies affixed to the church doors and in other suitable public places. Done at Loudun, July 2nd, 1634."

We may assume that this would end the disbelievers' doubts. It might have if nothing was done. Sister Claire, one of the possessed nuns, just as Père Lactance began his exorcism of her, confessed to the onlookers that she had lied about Urbain Grandier. She told of the coaching given her by Père Lactance, Mignon and some Carmelite brothers. They immediately said the devil was prompting this confession, and that she now lied. They took her away and locked her up. Next Mother Superior, dressed in bed clothes with a rope about her neck, interrupted a court examination of a nun by no less than de Laubardemont himself, saying she too had been coerced into lying. De Laubardemont said too that the devil in her was now speaking. Their ruse was now fully exposed.

Nevertheless within days the commission found Grandier guilty of crimes of magic, witchcraft and causing evil spirits to possess the Ursuline nuns and other females and causing other crimes to be committed. He was sentenced to be burned at the stake. Before the sentence was carried out he must tell who his accomplices were. To gain this knowledge, if he didn't speak freely, he would be tortured. He said he had no accomplices and was innocent of the accusations made against him.

On the day Grandier was to die, a surgeon was ordered to shave his entire body, for a devil could hide behind a single hair making him numb and free of any pain torture may cause. Orders were issued to yank his fingernails out, as a devil might hide there too. The surgeon refused. Finally he was taken to the provost's office which was filled with spectators, even ladies of quality, and presided over by M. de Laubardemont. An exorcism was performed, his sentence was read, stressing that extraordinary tortures were to be used. After the reading Grandier reaffirmed his innocence. De Laubardemont, thinking he feared the torturing, cleared the room except for two witnesses. Now he demanded the condemned man name his accomplices and sign a confession. Grandier refused and was turned over to his torturer, Père Lactance.

De Laubardemont ordered two boards placed between Grandier's legs just below the knees as well as a board on the outside of each leg then ordered them bound together. Two more boards were bound to these and wedges were pounded between the boards, one at a time. Each wedge took some pounding and with each blow Lactance demanded Grandier confess. During the time between each blow of the hammer or the addition of a new wedge the pain caused him to faint. They aroused him before continuing the torture. His legs were reduced to pulp, the marrow leaking through the binding cloth. A confession was placed before him to sign each time they revived him. He didn't sign.

Now unable to walk, he was tied to a board and returned to the provost's office. He asked a priest to hear his confession. This rite forbids the priest from ever telling what he heard. "Sign this confession first," said de Laubardemont pushing the paper at Grandier.

"Never, why after your torture should I sign? Only death awaits me."

"But," said his torturer, "We control how you die: slowly, quickly or in pain and agony." Grandier still refused.

When, after lying for hours in pain, he still refused to sign, he was carried out to the stake. He managed to beg a simple friar to ask the executioner to hurry his death. The friar tried by bribing the man. His sentence was read again and he was asked if the charges were true. He reiterated by asking to speak. This the exorcists did not want for they knew how good a speaker he was. When he started to speak they threw holy water in his face. Then one kissed him on the lips.

"The kiss of Judas," yelled Grandier.

For this he was struck in the face.

Grandier called out to the gathered people to pray for him.

Père Lactance grabbed a fistful of straw, dipped it in pitch and pushed it into the bound man's face screaming, "Confess!" Grandier resisted and Lactance threw more pitch on the wood and set it afire. The executioner was unable to reach the victim because of the flames. Doves were seen flying overhead. Some said they were there to carry him to heaven. Demons, said others, to carry him to hell. It was said that Grandier spoke to Lactance in that last moment, telling him he would die in thirty days. (He did.) Could this be true?

The servant shut the window cutting off the screams and blocking out the smoke.

Author's aside. If you are interested or curious about this story, I urge you to read Urbain Grandier, Celebrated Crimes by Alexandre Dumas.

Bye Jiminy

My story keeps me alive; however, as with all living things my time did come. It came about interestingly enough before my story was actually written. Let me tell you this: all living things have a place in heaven. I know, I'm here and this is how I got here.

I was sleeping near the hearth when a bright light lit up the room. I peered into it and thought I saw something at the workbench of the old man that lives in this house.

"I'll be damned. That is a Fairy and she has changed that wooden puppet into a live boy. Won't that surprise the old man. He goes to bed a lonesome old man and wakes up a father. By God, she spoke to the boy and he's answered her. How could he know a language already?"

Hopping over to see things up close, I didn't notice the old man get out of bed and begin hobbling over to check on the commotion. He was startled but very pleased that the Fairy had come to his house, and very disturbed to find a bug hopping quickly across the floor. I should have been paying attention, but a quick step and I was flattened under his shoe. Before I began my heavenly journey, I saw the old man scrape my remains off his size nine with a kindling stick and toss it into the smoldering embers in the fireplace.

You're Kidding

Chaplain Cooper, Royal Gunners Brigade, was being retired which deeply depressed him. Stepping from the steaming shower and wiping the mist from the mirror, he gazed upon himself, one of God's creatures.

His sagging abdomen hid his nonfunctional manhood. His thinning reddish hair standing up from the rubbing of the towel was nearly invisible. The whites of his eyes contained river tributaries of red, while beneath them two, no three, mail bag pouches hung. On either side of his head were reddening ears that Dumbo would envy. Plowed furrows crossed his forehead and the corners of his eyes looked like a flood plain delta.

He began laughing, letting the laugh roll out until he sat on the commode gasping for breath. He remembered he was made in the image of God and became convinced after seeing himself that his God had a very perverse sense of humor and laughed again.

Fishing

The breakfast dishes weren't finished and the heat slipped through every open cabin window. Laura and Linda, our six and four year old daughters were already carrying their poles toward the pier. Each had a tackle box, a net, a tin can of worms and a new fishing pole Santa brought last December. Sandals on their feet, hats at some angle indicating they weren't sitting correctly on top of their heads and a walk that showed the world they knew what they were doing completed the picture.

"Got worms?" I hollered from the screened-in porch.

"Daddy. You promised. No help, no questions. Remember, you promised."

I waved and went back in for my coffee. "OK, I promised. Wipe the look off your face."

My knowing wife nodded, and looked out the small window while wiping her hands on a floral towel. "If we sit on the porch with our coffee we can watch. Quiet as mice."

Both girls had begged, yes begged, for the opportunity to fish from the boat by themselves. It would remain tied to the dock. It had rained during the night and the boat listed a bit from the collected rainwater. I told them the boat couldn't be used today, but they could fish with their own worms in their own way from the pier. Neither mom nor I would bother them. They had total independence. We had pride.

The girls moved about the dock, some movements we understood, others needed interpretation. One or the other shook the can of worms over the pier bench while kneeling over it. Their shoulders, elbows and wrists were moving up and down and around in awkward disjointed motions. Then they stood along the pier and cast their line out, reeling in rather quickly and went back to kneeling at the bench.

"More coffee?" I was asked.

Turning, I held the cup up and felt it move out of my hand. "Sure."

Both of us were looking elsewhere, not at the kids on the pier. We jumped as we heard Laura shouting.

"Help! Help!"

She had fallen into the water. That quick. Turn your head and in an instant you may have a problem. The problem was shouting from the water. I was off the porch running the twenty feet or so to the end of the pier before the echo of her scream could have answered. Her mother was right behind me and several people emerged from other cabins reacting very quickly to the shouting.

I could see her wet head just above the end of the pier and jumped to the side of it. Landing in the water I grabbed her body with both hands picking her up at the same time. In my mind I knew something was wrong. The scene was wrong, all wrong.

Ah ha. The little light went on in my brain. *You are standing in water not quite up to your crotch. Laura's head, when she is standing, is higher than my belt. She had only to stand and she would not be drowning. Her screams were of fright, and our actions responded to her call.*

Lifting her onto the pier where she stood with several people who had answered her calls. She looked wide eyed at me then to her mother and the other folks standing about. I was about to scold her for her carelessness when I heard, "Daddy saved me. He's my hero."

Standing in the shallow water, feeling silly, how could I scold a little girl that moments ago thought her world was ending? Or who praised me as her hero. I blushed.

Destiny, A Woman's Creation

Eric Holiday's deep voice reached out to the students perched in a variety of positions around the outdoor koi pond. It's too nice to sit in a classroom they were told. So he walked them out of the building, across the library lawn and they settled down on the grass surrounding the pond. Sociology can be a very dull, boring, statistical class, but Mr. Holiday created situations and problems requiring his students to seek practical solutions. Right now he was presenting the class their latest assignment. It called for opinions and not necessarily facts. Hearsay, gossip and propaganda were acceptable.

"Write this down. The yellow race will rule the world, or a statement very similar, sounded throughout the world during the early stages of World War II. It was said by the Japanese who were then winning the war in the Pacific, and by the disillusioned, then losing the war. As the tide turned and the Japanese finally lost, the statement faded and became a rare memory. But, today the yellow race is emerging and one day will rule the world."

The following week he read one student's paper.

The yellow race will rule the world, or a statement very similar, sounded throughout the world during the early stages of World War II. It was said by the Japanese who were then winning the war in the Pacific, and by the disillusioned, then losing the war. As the tide turned and the Japanese finally lost, the statement faded and became a rare memory. But, the yellow race is emerging and one day will rule the world.

It's true. It is destiny. Women are creating this emerging ruling race. There is nothing wrong with this race and perhaps the world will be better for it. Much better, believe me.

It is the desire to be a mother that guides us toward this ultimate change. It is a woman's desire to mother a child. Not give birth, for some, an impossibility, but to nurture and love a child.

I cannot say how often men and women pester and beg, promise and scold their mate for a child. Finally, when all seems lost, they adopt. The child may not be of their race. Who cares? It is a child, someone to love and give family values, hope and a future. For the most part, from my point of view, it is educated white women with no financial worries that are doing the single parent adopting. Boy or girl, black, yellow or red, usually healthy, but not always, these women cover the globe looking for an unwanted child to raise and love.

They're wonderful people. Gentle, kind, devoted and brave, they're the movers and shakers of our changing world.

There are other women, those who can bear children, who are also changing the destiny of the world. They are the creators of the new yellow race. At one time their children were shunned, buried in the bottom rungs of society, even killed. These we called mulattos.

White slave owners created them with black women to enrich themselves by selling their progeny into slavery.

Today we know better. That is, if the woman says no to your sexual advances and you don't abide with her refusal, it's rape.

Any woman that willingly accepts a man from a different race may bear his offspring. There are genetic changes in their creation. Modified human changes that produce a child who is a little different from themselves. That is normal. We note the similarities in a newborn child, father's nose, mother's eyes, etc. Having mixed race relatives, I've never heard skin color mentioned at family gatherings. Light skinned, thin lips, narrow nose, kinky hair and other comparisons I've heard mentioned, but not yellow skin. Never mulatto.

Is the mulatto child accepted? Is their acceptance without the laws of our land being invoked? Do we still shun the child? From what I've seen we do not.

Perhaps the most visible acceptance is before us every day. We turn on the television set and the yellow race child stands before us. They are the pitchmen for products, the deliverers of the daily news and the heroes of our TV programs. We don't question their existence or the positions they hold. We don't see them as a threat as in W.W.II. They are our neighbors, our co-workers, our friends. They are the destiny of our world.

Putting the paper aside, Eric Holiday stood and stretched as he paced before the class. "Anyone care to comment on what was written?"

The Lesson

"Run Cindy, run. Hurry! Hurry!"

Cindy, running as fast as she could, looked like she wasn't moving. Her short legs taking her longest step didn't cover much ground. The fear in her heart pumped her muscles into a frenzy. She couldn't look back while she hustled across the field toward the fence. She knew McGruter's bull had mayhem in mind as he thundered closer behind her.

"C'mon Cindy!" Lucy screamed. "C'mon!"

Lucy, the ten-year-old ringleader of the foray into the McGruter pasture to collect hickory nuts, had gotten through the fence before the others. She stood next to the fence pole, one hand pulling a strand of barbed wire up and her foot pushing down on another strand of barbed wire. Her urgings for Cindy didn't overcome the fear of the charging bull. She held her position until

Cindy and the bull were close. In her mind too close. Lucy stepped back from the fence just as Cindy hurled herself through the opening.

The wires snapped shut, raking across the front and back of the flying Cindy. Yelps burst from pumping lungs. Pain fired from every nerve as the barbs dug into the passing flesh. The nuts, which Cindy had clung to as she ran, came tumbling out of the folds of her blouse, small bouncing brown nuggets of treasure rolling along the ground.

"Oh shit."

Not one of the four girls noticed Lucy's ejaculation. The reason was blood. Cindy's body oozed blood from all over. Their cries tempered the air with concern. Immediately they clustered round the girl, wondering what to do and doing nothing.

"You guys go home. Don't say nothing to nobody. OK?" the ringleader asked.

Mumbled responses came from bodies departing the scene, none protesting the order. "Cindy, come on home with me. I can use some of Mom's stuff and fix you up."

"It hurts."

"It must. I'm sorry I let loose of the fence wire. Guess I got scared. Sorry."

"I know. But my legs didn't move fast enough. Gosh, I was scared."

"Me, too."

The two girls headed for Lucy's house. Cindy limped a bit and cried a bit as they walked along. Neither the ten year old, nor the eight year old had a plan to cover the present situation. Trouble had a habit of finding them and now walked with them in silence.

Lucy went into the house first. Her father was flat out on the sofa watching something interesting to him on the television. He didn't rise or turn toward the two girls as they came into the foyer.

"Hi, Dad."

"Hi, Honey. Who's with you? Cindy?"

"Yeah. We're going to go play for a while in my room. OK?"

"Sure." He waved his arm as both girls scurried passed the door opening and clambered up the stairs. "Cut down on the noise, or Cindy goes home. Understand?"

"OK, Daddy. We'll be quiet."

Upstairs the conspirators went to work. Lucy's mom was a nurse. Her stuff was iodine, Mercurochrome, band-aids and salve. Cindy held up her blouse and Lucy took a long cotton swab and poked every bloody spot she saw. Then Cindy dropped her pants and they pock marked her legs.

That evening Cindy sat very still during the meal, then announced she would shower and get ready for bed. Not that she was going to bed, but would put on pajamas and loll around. She phoned Lucy, telling her the cuts hurt but her folks knew nothing, so far. The wounds kept her from sleeping. The morning announced, painfully, that today wouldn't be a good day for her, her friends or mom. Mom did want to know why on such a hot day she chosen to wear jeans.

"Just want to," came across as too flippant an answer.

"Don't answer in that manner, young lady."

"I just wantta wear jeans today that's all."

"Shorts will be cooler, but do what you want."

Cindy started through the door. "Going to Lucy's. See ya."

"Home by noon, you have a doctor's appointment."

Cindy died. She couldn't have an appointment today. He'd see everything. Mom would see everything. She thought of thousands of things on the way to Lucy's. None solved her dilemma. Lucy suggested running away, but nixed the idea at once. They tried dozens of stories, but none sounded truthful. The phone rang and Lucy's mom came to tell Cindy she was going to be late for the doctor's visit. Tempus fugit.

Cindy was quiet in the car and very quiet sitting in the waiting room. Perhaps worrying keeps some people quiet. She hoped when the nurse called her name, she'd be told the doctor was called to the hospital and she could go home. He was waiting for her. Doctor Lollard delivered Cindy and knew she had her quirks. He didn't expect her request she came into the room and sat on the examination table.

"Mom, can I be with the doctor alone please."

"Huh?"

"I want to talk to the doctor by myself. OK? Please?"

"OK, Cindy." The doctor said, walking to the door. "Go wait outside mother. Your daughter wants to talk to the doctor. Alone." Shutting the door he returned and stood, "Well, what's the problem?"

Cindy gave him a woe-begotten look and pulled up her shirt. "I don't want mom to know I got these."

"Hmmm…Cuts." He touched one, "Where did these come from?"

"McGruter's pasture fence. Yesterday." She winced as Doctor Lollard continued to touch several more reddened marks.

"Cindy, we have…No you have a problem. You have some infected cuts that need treatment. Tetanus shot for sure." He poked into a cabinet drawer. Your mom has to know."

"Does she? She'll kill me."

"These cuts can kill you if they aren't treated."

Cindy had permission to talk to Lucy that evening, after her mom told Lucy's mom what had happened. The mothers agreed some punishment would be handed out to both girls. Grounded for the weekend they tried to talk longer without success.

Monday came and both had nothing more to do than hike over to the McGruter fence and collect the lost booty of nuts. They were cautious, keeping an eye on the fence, and rewarded with most of the nuts. The nuts were delicious. The memory of how good they were sent both girls back the following year. However, they carefully checked out the field for a bull before scampering through the fence.

Pull

"Congressman Plaka, do you still believe you'll be reelected to Congress?" one of the reporters standing on the courthouse steps yelled.

"Certainly. I work very hard for my constituents and they recognize that."

"You think they will vote for you after your guilty verdict today?" the man shoving the microphone into the Congressman's face asked.

"Yes. Yes I do believe so. They know I will remain their voice in government."

Questions hollered in, but Plaka pointed to a young woman in the front of the group. "You have the last question."

"Well, Congressman. How can you be so sure?" came the quiet question.

"Young lady, now that this interview is over, get your cameraman to focus on the word on the handle of the door as you leave the building. It will tell you how I keep my job."

During the evening news the viewers were treated to a close-up shot of the one word embossed on the door handle **PULL**.

It seems a good explanation of how some politicians remain in office.

Don't That Beat All

Jimmy Sparrow, Lenny Brawn and Shadow Long were all yammering at once as their car sped along old Highway 14. The blue and red lights from the car pursuing them bounced off every object they touched. Neither the pursuing police nor the fleeing bank robbers were able to change the distance between them. The situation had to change. Soon.

"Jimmy, I can see the rail yard ahead," Shadow half yelled to the crouching driver.

"I can too. So what?" growled the impatient, panicking young crook. "We gonna take a train ride?"

"Hey, I'm being helpful. Several sets of tracks cross the highway there. If there's an engine moving boxcars around maybe we can get by and the cops is stuck by them."

"And if there ain't?" Lenny asked, his eyes probing the distant horizon for police.

"Then I duck behind something and we all run like hell. Every man for himself," the driver said. "Can't split the loot now. Shadow, you got the bag, hang on to it and we'll meet at my place tomorrow."

"Look! Look! There's an engine moving toward us now," Lenny squealed.

Sparrow sighed, "Good, we get a break. I'll swing in front of it, and the cops'll have ta stop."

"I see 'em."

Jimmy looked into the rearview mirror. Shadow turned to look through the back window with Lenny. Just ahead the road curved to the right. The engineer blew the whistle for the crossing much earlier than usual perhaps anticipating the speeding car was going to dart in front of it.

"We're gonna make it! We're gonna make it!" Jimmy Sparrow sang out. Without touching the brakes he swung the car hard to the right. He knew they would clear the tracks before the cops could catch up.

Later, the local TV news cameras and a reporter talked over the accident with a police officer. Before speaking on camera the police and paramedic crews compared notes. The conclusion reached for their reports was this; in pursuit of a car of suspected bank robbers, the pursued drove their car into a string of flat cars the engine was pushing. Three unidentified occupants were killed.

This story originally appeared in the Willow Review, 2008. This version has been modified.

Just for a Lark

The charged atmosphere surging through the passengers crowded into the railroad cars was unavoidable. The car John was standing next to was jammed with Union soldiers in a holiday mood shouting and yelling, four of the soldiers standing on the car platform were pleading for him to board. The train clattered backward, then forward, beginning the trip to its eventual destination.

"Come on, John, you shouldn't miss it."

"It will be a once in a lifetime experience. Unforgettable."

"I have no ticket," John hollered back.

"John, get on. We will outfit you in a uniform and you'll not be needing a ticket."

"Come on, we're moving," one hollered. "Come on."

Two uniformed arms with different rank markings reached out, grabbing John's elbows, lifting him off his feet and onto the lower step of the platform. John clutched the handrail as a resounding cheer from the surrounding soldiers nearly drowned out the screaming engine whistle.

The excitement continued as the rowdy group rode to their destination. A uniform made up of clothing from several men had a comic theatrical quality on the reluctant man. Yes he was with friends, but their enthusiasm wasn't infectious. John disembarked the train and joined their ranks as they assembled at the depot and marched off with them as the headed for their assigned place. When they finally came to a halt his heart nearly stopped at the sight before him.

The gallows frame filled the narrow area just off the road. You couldn't miss it and you couldn't tear your eyes from it. It stood there. Just stood there. God it was awful.

"A man's gonna die there, Geez."

"Come on men, get together. Look a little like soldiers. You there, get over here!"

"That damn thing isn't going to hold up to hang a man." I didn't move.

"Soldier I told you, move over here. Now!" hollered the Sergeant.

"Look at the old dry wood they used, and it's so poorly put together."

"Soldier, get into line. We need formation. Proper like."

"Lord those steps aren't nailed down just laid across. Piss poor apparatus for hanging a man."

"Attention!" bellowed the Sergeant, becoming angrier by the men's demeanor.

"Poor bastard, there isn't enough rope there for his neck either."

Again the Sergeant yelled out, "Listen you, I said, attention. Now do it."

"That's s a big man they're hanging. From here the hole looks too small to drop through."

"ATTENTION! ATTENTION!!! You wanna be put on report? ATTENTION!"

I hadn't realized the Sergeant was ordering me to move. My mind remained fixed on the gallows. *"What is it about watching a man die? Why did I think I'd wanna see it?"*

"Soldier, stand to or be reported."

"Sergeant what's going on here?" an approaching officer asked.

"Sir, it's him," his finger picked John, the created soldier, the casual standing, preoccupied and deep in thought, out of the line of men. "Washington sent these men down and I don't think they're prepared for this. Hell, excuse the language Sir, but he don't even look like a soldier."

The officer stepped before John, "This is an orderly hanging of a convicted traitor. John Brown committed treason!" He stepped away from the men, ran his eyes from one end of the line to the other, "As soldiers it's our duty to see the sentence carried out. Stand at attention!"

The line of men responded, stiff, upright soldiers, except for John. He tried, but the comical uniform seemed to prevent his looking like a soldier at attention. Once more the officer advanced toward John. "For the record solider, what is your name?"

"Booth, Sir. John Wilkes Booth!"

For the record. It has been told many times that when the soldiers were sent from Washington to control any possible trouble at John Brown's hanging, they encountered John Wilkes Booth at the railroad station. A few of the soldiers were friends of his and convinced him to accompany them and observe the hanging. As he had neither ticket nor permission to ride this train, he was disguised in a Union uniform. Not being a soldier, he would not have behaved as a soldier should. And as all the men admired him, they may have behaved a bit improperly. If the story is true, I don't know. Could it have happened? You judge.

Talk, Talk, Talk

The weather made Benjamin choose to ride the suburban train from the 75th Street Station instead of from 79th. He avoided boarding suburban trains at the Grand Crossing Station at 75th because of the police station. But today Tiny was sending him downtown to see Ralph the watch repair guy that had fooled Benjamin last year into thinking he was carrying thousands of dollars worth of diamonds. He knew what he was getting this time.

"Benjamin," said the man getting out of the car he just parked at the curb. "Passing by without saying hello?"

Benjamin turned slightly to see Patrolman "Swede" Olson locking his car door.

"Hi, I didn't notice it was you. I'm sortta in a hurry. Going downtown for Tiny."

"No. You didn't recognize me?"

"Wasn't paying attention I guess."

"Benjamin my good friend, there's another train in half an hour. Tiny, doesn't have you working by the clock does he?"

"Nope. But he would like me to hurry." Benjamin didn't like the idea of missing the train. And he wasn't sure why Swede wanted to talk to him in the station. "Really, I'd like to make this train. You don't need me for something do you?"

The hand on his shoulder proceeded to ease him along the street back toward the police station. The smoothness of the effort had trapped Benjamin into joining the officer in a lock step fashion right into the Grand Crossing Police Station. He was going in whether he wanted to or not.

The deskman looked up, nodded to Swede and asked, "Bringing him in?"

"No. I'll check in then I'll ask Benjamin a few questions and he can go." He pointed to a chair, "Just be a minute. You stay and wait for me. OK?"

"OK," in a tone spoken by a disillusioned person caught in the act of doing something wrong, "I'll wait. But kinda hurry, huh?" Can I get some water?"

"Help yourself. But stay out of his way."

The man bringing in the bottled water was working next to Benjamin. Two policemen passed holding onto a man they were walking toward the back of the building. One officer Benjamin recognized but didn't know his name. Another officer wearing a different uniform was also passing him. He carried a water cup just like Benjamin's.

The screaming and ruckus started immediately. It was the guy they were taking back to the cells. Everything was happening in front of Benjamin as he flopped back into the chair to get out of the way. Every little thing seemed to click into his memory like a camera taking pictures.

The guy had broken away from the two officers and was coming toward him. The deliveryman was turning the big bottle over when he was bumped sending water everywhere. The out of town cop tried moving to help by setting his cup on the small table next to the water bottle. Benjamin's cup was knocked loose spilling water all over the floor. The Swede moved in and punched the guy down, out cold. Calm returned at once.

"Benjamin, go on, catch your train. I'm going to be busy."

He got up and ran for the train. His shirt and pants were wet, but he made his train. It was about five or six hours later when he got back to the pool hall. The story was circulating at the pool tables and the card tables. Everyone was enjoying a good laugh. Benjamin asked Tiny what was going on. That started more laughter.

"Let me ask you something. Swede came in here about ten minutes ago looking for you. Said he wanted to talk to you. You got trouble with that guy?"

"No. I don't think so."

"Well I'm telling you if you think you are, go to a movie or stay some where else tonight."

"Honest, Tiny I got no trouble with him. When I was going to get your watch... Oh, here it is." He handed Tiny the package Ralph gave him earlier. "On my way to the train, he took me into the police station."

"He did? Why? You ran out on him? Did you?"

"No, no. Honest. They had some guy start a fight and Swede told me to leave on account a he thought he had troubles and didn't need me."

"Well you better sta..."

"Benjamin, I want to see you." The Swede had returned.

"Hey, you told me I could go. Remember?"

"Benjamin, Benjamin. I did tell you to go. Now I'm telling you to stay. I need to talk to you. Come on outside. We can talk really quiet."

"I didn't do nothing. Come on. I don't even know anything."

"Benjamin, I promise you... Here, Tiny, listen to my promise.

Benjamin, I promise to only talk to you. Something funny happened and maybe you can tell me how."

Tiny was giggling. "Very funny." He laughed, "Go, nothing's gonna happen. Get Swede to talk before you talk." The entire pool hall crowd heard Tiny's remark and exploded with laughter. Poor Benjamin, confused and perplexed tentatively walked out in front of the Swede.

"Come on kid, we'll just walk," he turned left, "and I want you to tell me what you saw happen at the station before I told you to go get your train."

"Huh?" Now he was confused and his face wrinkled in bewilderment. "I saw?"

"Before or during the fight in the station, did you see anything happen?"

"Are you trying to trick me or some..."

"No tricks, I promised. Did you... no. What did you see happen? Just tell me what happened when that guy started the ruckus. OK?"

"Well this guy broke away, I guess, from the guys taking him to a cell. He started to run passed me for the door and you decked him. One punch and down and out."

"You saw that?" Swede seemed to smile as he asked, "See anything happen before then? Think Benjamin, think. I really need the information. Maybe whatever you saw will help. From the time we walked in, do you remember anything that you saw?"

The camera-like film began popping pictures into his head. "Yeah, I remember seeing lottsa things. It's sortta funny, I see what's going on like in a movie. You want to hear me tell you that?"

"You bet. Everything, I won't interrupt you either."

"Well when we came in the desk man asked if you were booking me. You said no and I sat down. There was a guy delivering water and I asked if I could get a drink. You said yes and not to leave." Benjamin paused, "OK? That what you want me to remember?"

Swede nodded.

"OK," Benjamin warmed to the task. "I see the guy is about to dump the new bottle into the cooler and he nods for me to get mine first and step outta the way. As I get my water these two guys, officers, are taking a guy back to the cells. And one of your guys and an out of town cop walk by. The out of town fella is carrying a water cup just like mine. Then there's hollering and the arrested guy is running toward me. I fall back into my chair, and as the guy runs by me you punch him." Stopping, Benjamin gave Swede a half smile, one to prompt approval. "That's it."

"Benjamin, some other things mustta happened. Think. I can't prod your memory, but I just know if you saw all that, you saw more. Come on, think hard, remember some other things maybe."

Their walk had circled back to Cottage Grove near the theater. "Look, here's the candy shop. Want some ice cream? My treat. But you gotta tell me more. Hell you can tell me the same story again and you might add something."

"A sundae."

"Yeah, a sundae."

Sitting in the booth across from each other, Swede watched Benjamin poke a monstrous helping of ice cream into his mouth. "You can't talk with your mouth full. Go slow and talk to me as you eat."

The answer from Benjamin was muted, the smile a pleasure. He gulped then went on with his story of what he saw, repeating many things. There were a few different items mentioned. "The jail breaker, he gets charged for that, don't he?"

"Attempted."

"The jail breaker bumps the guy with the water bottle and the jug starts splashing water. I'm falling into the chair and my water is dropped. That out of town policeman tried to put his water on the table. I think he was gonna help stop the jail breaker. I ain't sure. His cup spills. You know I'm sure his cup spills into the water cooler. There's some sliding around and you punched the guy. One punch, down and out cold."

"That's what you saw happen. You saw the officer's cup of jui...water spill into the water cooler? You actually saw that happen?"

"Un, huh. Into the water, that important? Was it poison or something?" There was an edge of excitement in Benjamin's question.

"Well, sort of. Not real poison and not enough kill anyone. I'm going to tell you only after you swear to me you will not tell anyone my story."

"No one? I can't tell nobody?" Benjamin asked with a frown. "OK. Tell me your story. Is that why the guys in the pool hall are all laughing?"

They were walking back toward the pool hall now. Swede waved to a passing squad car when it sounded its horn. "Here is what may have happened and with your story, I am sure it will go in the record book. The out of town officer, Juan Perdo, is up here to pick up a prisoner and take him back to Florida, then he'll be sent to Cuba. This guy is into occult stuff."

"What's occult?"

"That, Benjamin is like religious stuff, or voodoo in the movies, only it's more weird. Anyway, Officer Perdo mixed up some juice from one of the plants they call Dumb Cane in the Chief's office... He gonna give it to this guy. It makes a person lose their voice. Perdo thought that since his man believed in voodoo he might think after Perdo told him liars lose their voices once a spell is cast on them, he might talk. The juice was in the water cup he had and when he put it down it must have spilled into the water cooler. He thought it went on the floor.

Later on some of the officers, visitors and clients started losing their voices. Scared the hell out of everybody. Fortunately Perdo had already left with his guy. Unfortunately, most of us didn't know about it and thought someone poisoned the water. Coolidge was with Perdo and he talked to the Chief, and he calmed everyone down. Some of the officers went over to Jackson Park Hospital. No one there knew what to make of it. When word got out everyone started laughing at us 'cause we made fools of ourselves."

"Did you think I did it?"

"No Benjamin. I never thought you would do something like that. I thought you might have seen someone or something that could explain what happened. You did and thanks. I'll remember you helped me. See you," said Swede turning to walk toward the station. "Remember, you tell no one."

Benjamin walked into pool hall wondering how he could avoid telling why the Swede wanted him. Tiny was in the can and the card and pool players paid no attention to Benjamin walking by. He went upstairs and went to bed.

Timing

Alonzo packed his sample bag in the trunk of the car then finished writing the order before phoning in to the main office. Looking at his watch he noticed it was later than usual for his daily visit, but time was important, mom could wait. She was always there in her own world often unaware that he was with her. He stopped to order a burger and coke devouring them as he drove to the hospital. At the hospital he used the men's room, tidied up and decided for health reasons to walk up to the third floor.

The hospital attendant paused in her bed making when Alonzo stepped into the room. "There's no one here, Sir."

"I see. Where is she?"

"They took her out a few minutes ago sir. She died."

Paid in Full

Bert Shuman, looking into Roman Buterio's eyes and feeling his body blacking out as his windpipe was being crushed, believed every word the man said. He heard the words again, coming out of his mouth as he awoke in the alley behind the liquor store. "Get me my money, or you're dead meat."

Bert Shuman once considered his future assured, but had gambled it away. His house, business, insurance policy, car and jewelry, even the annuity left by his mother and the trust fund she left for the grandchildren. Where could he get over a hundred grand? He seriously contemplated suicide before walking out of the alley. But fate saved his miserable ass. As he exited the garbage-strewn alley the flashing neon sign, Pat's Place, caught his eye.

Pat, the wife he deserted twelve years ago, the mother of the children whose trust fund he'd stolen, was the woman he once insured for a million dollars, double indemnity. God, he thought, get rid of her, pay Buterio and have enough left to live well again. He called on the policy and found it was still valid and he was still the beneficiary. He audaciously called Pat and found her home and willing to see him. Their meeting was amiable, with some tears and memories clouding some of their talk. They agreed to meet again, the day after tomorrow, at Lindsey's for a six o'clock dinner.

Plans, he had none at all. He knew she must die for him to collect, how to accomplish this gave Bert nightmares and daymares, if there's such a word. Without a doubt he had to get into the house and create an accident and the sooner the better. He must stay overnight, kill her and say a robber did it. Weak. Hire someone to run her down in traffic. Weak. Every idea appeared to be weak, flawed and impossible. Then, as they dined he saw a clear, simple method. Pat couldn't handle a drink, never could. He would get her drunk some night, leave the car motor running in the garage and asphyxiate her.

Pat didn't object to his suggestion of staying overnight, but not in her bed. Agreed. Bert requested a dip in the warm water of the spa. He and Pat listened to Sonny and Cher music, their old favorite on the high-fi system Pat had installed after Bert walked out on her and the kids. Stepping out of the tub Pat began swearing at Bert, calling him every name she could think of and ended it with a simple statement.

"I haven't forgotten a certain insurance policy that leaves a million dollars to the survivor after the first of us dies you son of a bitch. Thanks for a million bucks."

Pat shoved the high-fi into the pool. The investigator told Pat how foolish she had been, leaving the equipment on a weak support so close to the water, and how lucky she was that she wasn't in there when the accident happened. The police investigating cleared her of any wrongdoing and the insurance company paid double indemnity for the accident. Her children plan to attend college, while Roman Buterio cussed the loss of a hundred and forty grand.

A Fly on the Wall

A fly on the wall is often suggested to open a discussion.

Suppose a fly sitting on the wall overheard the first plotters discuss the assassination of Julius Caesar. Who were these instigators? Who drew in friend Brutus?

Why was it planned to time with the Ides? Did the Oracle actually warn Caesar, or is this pure Shakespeare? How could this great soldier and leader allow himself to blunder into such a trap? Were there other co-conspirators? The fly on the wall knows no names. It can be said that names are unimportant.

The deed? The deed is entirely different.

These noble men in senatorial robes trimmed with royal purple clenched their angry fists and vowed vengeance for deeds they thought would imperil their positions in Rome. Did they know or understand the great Caesar's intentions? I think not.

Bent close, their heads nodded in agreement to each other's claim of injustice. The nucleus of treason budded there. The conspirators meet secretly. Perhaps they could save face. Who knows? In ancient Rome leaders often killed their enemies, or possible enemies. They didn't think twice about it or their enemies would kill them.

The fly followed and listened as they hatched their deadly plot. Were these plotters any different than the group that assassinated leaders and thus changed history?

"We must bring someone Caesar trusts," said one of the original plotters.

Each face examined a face and though unspoken asked, "Who?" One of his aides? No. A general? No. Who is willing and close enough to consider killing Caesar?

"Assassination!" The word crept into each mind. Did anyone consider the enormity of this deed?

Wishing to hear better, the fly flew closer. SMACK!!! Someone crushed it.

Prairie Voices

Ian Welch, an environmental engineer, felt one leg of his surveying equipment strike something hard. Kicking it, he loosened a charred fragment of wood attached to a rusted piece of metal. Ian recognized the object as part of a very old wagon wheel spoke and rim. Knowing this area of the prairie never felt the stress of civilization, he wondered how and what caused it to be partially burned and buried here. Squatting down, Ian imagined a possible scenario that left the small piece of civilization on vast vistas of a lonely prairie.

A hawk's talons pinned a prairie dog to the ground, its squeals carried on the wind through the rustling dry grass. Young prairie chicks paraded behind a clucking hen now stopping to scratch the hardened soil for sustenance. A dove's mournful notes called out searching for a mate. Adding to these came the heavy rumble of covered wagons, the hoof steps of tired horses, their leather harnesses rubbing together, the crack of a whip and the sounds of people talking. The sounds blended into the voice of the 1878 prairie.

Moses Kohler, leaning out from the seat of the lead wagon, pointed a finger to the northwest. "Jim, look over there." Growing dark clouds attracted the old man's attention. "You think that storm is coming this way?"

"Could. I've been out on the prairie during a storm, they're really bad." Jim Blucher, hired scout for the wagon train, stood in his stirrups straining for a better view. "I'm guessing it's coming and we haven't time to protect ourselves."

"How much time do you think Jim?"

"Well those cloud towers are growing as I look. Maybe we got an hour—maybe less. Either way we ain't got much time."

Moses reined in his team. "Better get the men up here. We need some serious planning and quick."

The wagons following Moses stopped when he did. Jim gave a *come-up-here* wave of his arms and shouted. "Isaac, Jubal, we got to talk, get on up here. Now."

Jim had only three wagons left in his train. Three wagons of the Kohler family, eleven people heading toward the Columbia territory. They left St. Louis with an even dozen wagons the last week of June. One wagon never started and to Jim's dismay he lost two more wagons the first week. Rolf Verbal's wife, expecting their first child, became very ill. She pleaded with Rolf to take her back to St. Louis, telling him she needed bed rest or she'd lose the unborn child. Amy Stevens, also expecting a child, convinced her husband to turn back too.

Four weeks later, Jim's group met with a train of nine wagons heading south. There were still rumors of gold being found in the west. Four wagons joined the group headed south, but agreed not to ask Jim to return the cash paid in advance for his services. The entire trip stopped to bury Selma and Gregory Oates, who were killed when their team broke loose, flipped their wagon over and crushed them. Not that he wanted the thought, but it flashed into his mind; would this advancing storm wipe out the last of the Jim Blucher train?

Four men gathered in front of Moses' team, watched the darkening sky and saw several bright lightning strokes crossing from horizon to horizon. Fear showed on each man's face. Jim ordered the livestock and horses staked away from wagons. Jubal volunteered his wagon be emptied and tied down with the women and children hidden beneath it, the men huddling down as close as they could next to the wagon. Moses, the patriarch, assured everyone the storm wouldn't last long but they must stay together.

"I think we're ready," Moses said as a strong gust of wind carried his words away.

"Down! Everyone grab hold to anything solid, try and lock your arms and legs into any rope or space," yelled Jim trying to get one more view. "Hold tight and pray to God."

The earth started vibrating. A deafening roar grew in intensity and the rushing wind brought a new warning to the huddled people. Smoke. Somewhere the grasses had ignited from a bolt of lightning. The inferno encouraged by the howling wind drove the massive herds of buffalo before it. Flames licking the dry grass soared higher and higher. No barrier withstood their fear-crazed flight. Fallen beasts trampled by the stampeding herd became bloody blots upon the ground. The standing wagons filled with supplies and family belongings flew along on the backs and horns of the thundering bovines, then fell beneath their hooves in tiny pieces. The protective wagon bed splintered into shards, the screams of the trapped Kohler family never reaching beyond the racing winds.

When the rain finally soaked the tattered remnants, the blood of man and animal was washed away. Little showed of the drama that just occurred. Before the sun set that evening, a magnificent rainbow divided the sky gradually fading as night settled across the blackened stubble. A few prairie dogs crawled out of collapsed tunnels and barked greetings to one another. A lone owl hooting in passing flight was joined by the distant yelping of a scavenging coyote. A slight breeze rustled a few blades of unburned grass missed by the fire rapid passage. The animals and the wind, as they did for eons, continued producing the sounds of the prairie's night voices.

ABOUT THE AUTHOR

I am the first born son of a sixteen-year-old high school drop-out. For most of my first seven years, relatives took care of me, and the next eight years Catholic Charities sheltered, fed, clothed and guided me. I dropped out of school and started working one month after I turned sixteen.

Married at twenty-one, with a child on the way, I decided to return to school, but there was a hitch. I worked as a clerk on the railroad during the evening hours, so night school was out. Instead, I attended school during the day as a regular student. It took from 1951 until 1964 to get a Master's Degree. Incidentally, I've taken a class in something every year since 1951.

I became a teacher, then a naturalist and back to teaching junior high science until I retired. I retired early due to Parkinson's Disease, which effected my ability to read and write notes on student's papers. I have taught at every level from preschool to college. After retiring, I tried professional bowling. I found more success as an artist. A story of my early childhood is in the Willow Review, 2005.

Printed in the United States
143981LV00001B/5/P

9 781933 449746